Just Plain Bob

The Hitch Hikers

10 XXX Explicit Stories

WARNING

This book contains sexually explicit scenes and adult language. It may be considered offensive to some readers. This book is for sale to adults ONLY.

Please store your files wisely where they cannot be accessed by underage readers.

* * * * * * * * * * * * * * * * * *

About the Publisher

4Fun Publishing, a member of **BLVNP Incorporated**, 340 S. Lemon #6200, Walnut CA 91789, info@blvnp.com / legal@blvnp.com
NOTE: Due to the highly emotional reaction of some people to works of erotic fiction, any email sent to the above address that contains foul language or religious references is automatically deleted by our anti-spam software and will not be seen. All other communications are welcome.

DISCLAIMER

Please don't be stupid and kill yourself. This book is a work of FICTION. Do not try any new sexual practice that you find in this book. It is fiction and not to be confused with reality. Neither the author nor the publisher or its associates assume any responsibility for any loss, injury, death or legal consequences resulting from acting on the contents in this book. Every character in this book is over 18 years of age. The author's opinions are not to be construed as the opinions of the publisher. The material in this book is for entertainment purposes ONLY. Enjoy.

The Hitch Hikers
10 XXX Explicit Stories

By: Just Plain Bob

© Just Plain Bob 2015
ISBN: 978-1-68030-629-3

The Hitch Hikers

Cookie

Debbie

Denise

Joyce

Lee Ann

Stephanie

Alice

Amy

Shauna

Elise

Hitch Hiker Cookie

We stopped for dinner and gas at a truck stop just outside of Wichita. We had been visiting Cookie's folks in Mulvane and we were headed back home to Denver. I was looking forward to getting home to my own bed and not just because I wanted to sleep. Cookie's parents live in a house with paper-thin walls and Cookie wouldn't let me make love to her there. I had slept next to her, but had gone without sex for the whole nine days we were there and I was hurting. I had pulled into a rest stop and had tried to get Cookie into the back seat, but she told me no, "I want it as bad as you do baby, but let's wait until we get home."

I had gotten up to use the bathroom and when I came back to the table Cookie wasn't there. I guessed that she had also gone to the bathroom, but when she hadn't come back after five minutes I began to wonder just where in the hell she had gotten to. I was just getting ready to get up and stick my head in the ladies room when the waitress came up to me and handed me a piece of paper.

"The lady you were with asked me to wait ten minutes and give this to you." I took it from her and saw that it was a note from Cookie to me.

"I've decided to give you the fantasy that you have always wanted. See you at home."

Give me my fantasy? I didn't have any fantasies. Why in the hell hadn't I been able to make her understand that? I sat in the booth another hour waiting for her to come back and then I went out to the car and waited another forty-five minutes before I accepted the fact that she wasn't coming back.

* * *

As I drove home to Denver alone I thought back to how it all had started. It had been my birthday and my younger brother Ron had given me a subscription to Penthouse Letters. I really had no interest in the magazine or its content, but when the issues began to arrive I read them. I didn't believe for one minute that the letters in the magazine were real or if they were written by idiots. Real people didn't say things like "magnificent fuck stick" or "marvelous meat pole." And none of the people were ugly or ordinary looking; everyone had larger than average cocks and the women were all drop dead gorgeous. They were good for a laugh and so I generally read most of the issue before tossing it out.

After about the fifth issue Cookie started asking me why I wasted my time reading such filth:

"Honestly Dave, I don't understand why you just don't toss that in the trash when it comes in."

Another month passed by and when the next issue arrived and Cookie saw me reading it she said:

"Is that garbage reaching you on some level? Is that why you read it? Do you find things in there that excite you? You are changing Dave; you aren't the man I married anymore."

* * *

I thought she was over-reacting. She came from a fairly straight-laced background and for the first two years of our marriage wouldn't even make love with the lights on. Things came to a head with the ninth issue. I was sitting on the living room couch reading it when Cookie came in and said:

"What is it Dave? Do you see me doing those things? Do you have some sick fantasy about seeing me or having me do the things described in that magazine? Is that it Dave? You want to watch me with another man? What is it Dave, you want to see me with a black man, maybe do a gangbang? Or is it another woman you want to see me with?

You are one sick puppy Dave" and she stormed out of the room leaving me sitting there wondering just what the hell happened. But her tirade told me something - she was reading the magazines, how else would she know the content?

I finally got tired of the bitching and when the next issue arrived I threw it in the trash unopened and I saw Cookie see me do it. The expression on her face was curious - it almost looked like she was upset. I had two issues left on the subscription and I told Cookie to throw them out when they came and I never saw them so I thought that she had. One day I was cleaning out the bedroom closet looking for some stuff to give to Goodwill and I moved a box on the top shelf. The box had some weight to it and I couldn't remember seeing it before so I opened it and looked inside. I found all twelve issues of Penthouse Letters - she had not thrown them away - she had even gone into the trash and retrieved the issue I had thrown away. At the time I didn't know what to make of it, but now on the drive home it dawned on me that it was Cookie who had the fantasies. She had finally decided to act on them and she was setting me up to take the blame if everything turned to shit.

* * *

I arrived home at seven o'clock on Friday night and I didn't hear from Cookie until five on Sunday afternoon. She asked me to come and pick her up and I almost hung up on her, but curiosity being what it is I had had to know what she had done. I pulled into the Denny's where she had asked me to pick her up and she came out of the restaurant before I even got the car parked. She slid onto the front seat, looked me right in the eye and said:

"Well, I hope you are happy now that I've debased myself for you and your perverted fantasies."

I ignored her, pulled out of the lot and headed for the house.

"I hope your warped little mind is ready for this. Since you would never tell me what your sick little fantasy was, I ended up doing them all.

Well, all except the one where you watch, but Phil says he will come over and do me while you watch if that's what you want."

"Phil?"

"The truck driver who picked me up while you were in the bathroom. He walked up to the table and told me he was headed for Denver and would sure like to have some pretty company along for the ride. I decided that if I was going to give you your fantasy then was as good a time as any. I'll say one thing for him, he sure didn't believe in wasting time. He had his cock out and in my mouth before you even got back to the table. He fucked me right there in his truck while I watched you sit at the table and wait to see if I'd come back. He fucked me three times before we even left the parking lot. I was sucking his cock when you started the car and left. We stopped five times on the way to Denver. I didn't think I'd ever be able to satisfy him.

"Just outside of Limon there was a black guy hitching a ride and I talked Phil into stopping and giving him a ride. He didn't want to, but I told him I would spend the weekend with him if he would. I got in the sleeper and when the black guy climbed up in the cab I got him to get in the sleeper with me. It's true what they say about black men Dave. He was huge! He fucked me three times before we let him out at Colfax and I-70. I never even knew his name."

I sat there behind the wheel and watched the road in front of me and tried not to scream at her to shut up, but I held my temper because I wanted to hear all of it.

"When we got to the terminal and dropped off his truck we got in his car and he took me home with him. I was surprised when we walked into his apartment and I found out that he was married. I was even more surprised when his wife smiled at me and said:

"I hope he told you that we share everything."

"It was my first time with a woman and I liked it. The three of us spent the night in the same bed, but none of us got much sleep. Saturday night Phil and Ava took me with them to a bar they go to and I had a little too much to drink. I don't remember much of it, but Ava told me that I got gangbanged on the back seat of her car by at least twelve guys, maybe more. All I remember is waking up between two guys in Ava's spare bedroom. They took turns fucking me most of the day and then Phil did me one last time before dropping me off at the Denny's. You must be pretty horny by now so let's hurry home so I can fuck your brains out."

I just shook my head and said, "It won't wash Cookie, it just won't wash. I never had any fantasies and you know it. The fantasies were all yours, not mine. I found the books in the closet - all twelve of them - and I know you read them all. Trying to pretend that you did it for me isn't going to work."

I pulled over and parked. Then I got out of the car and went around to her side, opened the door and pulled her out of the car.

"What are you doing Dave? What is this?"

"It's called a bus station" and I handed her a five twenties. "Catch a bus back to your parents or a cab to take you to Phil and Ava's, I don't much care which as long as I never have to look at your sorry ass again" and I drove off and left her standing there.

The phone is ringing again. It hasn't stopped for a week now. She calls four and five times a day, every day, begging me to take her back. I've gotten to where I don't answer it anymore. Tomorrow I think I'll have the number changed.

~~~***~~~

Hitch Hiker Debbie

I had stopped at a Tomahawk truck stop to get fuel and a bite to eat. I'd finished fueling and had gone inside and gotten a booth, ordered my meal and was sitting there sipping my coffee when a car pulled up and parked just outside my window. Normally I'm not a nosy person; I tend to mind my own business, but I just happened to be looking out the window as the car pulled up and I found myself looking at one of the most beautiful faces I had ever seen. Our eyes met and for a brief instant I could read her facial expression - it said, plain as day, "What the fuck are you looking at."

I went back to sipping my coffee, but a minute or so later I picked up some movement out of the corner of my eye and I looked out the window to see the woman slapping the driver's face. The passenger door flew open and the woman got out of the car, slammed the door and began walking toward the entrance of the restaurant. The guy in the car was staring at her with an "What the hell did I do?" look on his face and as I watched the expression changed to "Well, fuck you bitch!" Then the headlights came on and the car backed up and pulled out of the parking lot.

I had been looking out the window and I hadn't noticed the woman approach and I didn't realize she was there until I heard "that miserable son of a bitch" and I turned to see her standing next to my booth watching the car turn onto the highway. She said again, "That miserable bastard, that miserable no good rotten bastard!"

I looked up at her standing there and noticed that besides a drop dead gorgeous face she had a killer set of tits. My eyes dropped and confirmed that the rest of her was in keeping with the top half and while I was looking I heard her say, "You mind if I join you? It looks as if my darling husband has abandoned me."

I waved for her to take a seat and asked her if he did things like that often.

"This is the fourth time. He will go two or three exits down the road and then come back after making me wait around. He thinks he is showing me who is the boss. One of these days he's going to do it and I'm not going to be here when he gets back."

Just then the waitress brought me my hamburger steak and I ask the woman if she had eaten yet. She said no, picked up the menu and looked at it and then told the waitress that she would have what I was having. I pushed my food around on my plate as we waited for her meal to arrive and wondered if taking advantage of the situation might not be in my best interests; after all, I might never have a shot at something as nice as this ever again. She had said that someday he might come back and find her gone-- why not today? Her food came and we ate in silence; me thinking about how much I would like to have her in my sleeper cab and she no doubt thinking of ways to get even with her husband. I had just finished my meal and was trying to think of a clever way to approach the subject when she looked at me and said:

"You want to get lucky?"

Sometimes I can be a little slow on the uptake and I said, "Pardon me?"

She grinned, "I said do you want to get lucky?"

Suddenly it dawned on me that she had beaten me to the punch.

"If you are suggesting what I hope you are, you bet I would."

"Which way are you going?"

"To Denver."

"Do you have a sleeper on your truck?"

"Yes ma'am, I do."

"What are we waiting for?"

I threw enough money down on the table to cover both meals and the tip and said:

"Let's get the hell out of here before he comes back."

I was just pulling onto the highway when she pointed and said, "There he is."

I looked over at her and said, "Are you sure you want to do this?"

She looked undecided for a minute and then she said, "Fuck him! He's done this to me one too many times."

I pulled out on the highway and headed on down the road. We rode the first twenty minutes in silence and then I said, "I'm not holding you to what you said, the part about getting lucky. I know you were pissed at the time and you might not have really meant it."

She looked over at me, "I meant it."

"Well, that brings up something else. As soon as we get to Denver I drop the truck at the terminal and head home. Would you rather the sleeper or a bed?"

She looked at me and grinned, "Can't I have both?"

I smiled back at her and pulled off onto the next exit ramp and parked on the shoulder. I set the air brakes and turned on my blinkers and turned to her to say "After you" but I was talking to her back as she had already parted the curtain and was crawling up onto the mattress. She was down to her panties by the time I crawled in behind her and she chuckled,

"This is really going to piss him off. His biggest fantasy has been to watch me with another guy and here it is happening and he's not here to see it."

By the time she had finished telling me that I had my clothes off. She looked down at my stiff cock and said:

"Do you know that yours is the first cock I've seen since I married Harry ten years ago?" She reached over and took it in her hand, spread her legs and said, "Hurry, I want it."

As I entered her I warned her that I hadn't gotten laid in a while "so the first time might be quick, but I do recover quickly."

"No problem sweetie, we have all the time we need. I have no intention of going back to Harry until you have fucked me into exhaustion."

True to my prediction I only lasted about two minutes and I kind of left her hanging, but to make up for it as soon as I pulled my cock out of her I moved around and went down on her. It usually surprises girls when I go down on them just after I've shot my load in them and this one was no exception.

"You aren't going to do that, are you?"

I smiled up at her, "Yes ma'am, I am."

From the way she bucked and bounced around I think she liked it. Her hand reached out and grabbed onto my cock and she began pulling on it and it started to grow. She started tugging on it pretty hard so I swung up over her and she did something to me that no other girl had ever done - she licked it! She licked it like it was an ice cream cone; up one side and down the other and then back again. She licked the head, the shaft, and my balls for a good two minutes before she took me in her mouth. It wasn't long at all before I was hard enough for her again and this time she wanted to be on top. She bounced up and down on me for a good five or six minutes before I rolled her over and started fucking her as hard as I could. After a minute or so she cried out, "Oh Jesus, oh God" and she pulled me to her and held me tight as she had an orgasm and a few moments later she moaned, "Fuck me lover, fuck me" and I went back to banging her as hard as I could. She had one more orgasm and then I had mine and I rolled off of her. She reached out and touched my face:

"Maybe I should have done this sooner. Maybe I should have let my husband have his fantasy. I never knew I could enjoy another man so much. How soon can you go again?"

I smiled at her, "How quickly can you get me up?"

We stopped twice more before we got to my terminal and I dropped her at a Denny's because I'm not supposed to have anyone in the truck with me who is not a company employee. I honestly didn't expect to find her there when I got back, but there she was.

"I wondered if you would come back for me" and I laughed and told her that I'd had the same thought about her.

"You should have known I'd be here lover, I'm having too much fun and I'm going to have even more when I rub my hubby's nose in it."

We got in my car and headed off toward my apartment. We hadn't gone two blocks when she slid over next to me and reached for my zipper, "Do we have far to go or should we stop for a quickie?"

I laughed, "If you can't wait ten minutes I suppose I could pull over."

"I can wait ten minutes lover, but not much more than that."

Two more blocks and she had her head in my lap and she kept it there until we pulled in at my apartment. As we climbed the steps to my second floor unit she said, "How much time do I have?"

"What do you mean?"

"Do you have a wife or girlfriend, someone that I need to be gone before they come over?"

"Our only time table is whatever you want it to be. I have three days before my next trip and even then I have room in the sleeper if you want to come along."

"Really? Where do you go?"

"San Francisco, Los Angles, San Diego and then back to here."

As I was unlocking my door she said, "I might just take you up on that."

We made love three times and then fell asleep. I slept almost seven hours and when I woke up she was still lying next to me on the bed. I was looking down at her and thinking that her husband was a flaming idiot for letting her out of his sight and I was wondering if I should wake her up and have her call home before he called the cops and reported her missing. My thoughts were interrupted:

"Penny for your thoughts" and I looked down to see that she was awake.

"I'd need more than that because I was having more than one."

I told her what I had been thinking and she said, "The idiot might just do that. I guess I'd better call him."

I showed her where the phone was and watched while she punched in some numbers. There was a pause and then:

"Just calling to see if you were at home and to let you know that I might not be home for a while."

"No. A gentleman offered me a ride and since I didn't feel like sitting around waiting for you while you were off having your snit fit I said yes."

"No, I don't think so. He will probably bring me home when he gets tired of me."

"What? How should I know? Tonight, tomorrow, next week, whenever he gets tired of me."

"Of course I did."

"Yes."

"You bet. As many times as I want to or he wants me to."

"Well wait just a minute and I'll ask him."

She turned to me and said, "He's being an asshole. How would you feel about my moving in with you?"

I gave a big smile and she smiled back at me and said into the phone, "He thinks it's a great idea. I'll call you back in a week or so and see how you feel about it then" and she hung up.

She turned to me and said, "I love the asshole, but I'm tired of being taken for granted. I'll end up going home to him, but not until I've made him sweat. You've got me until it's time for your next trip and then I'll call him again and see how he feels. If he gives me a ration of shit you'll have me for company on your run. How does that sound?"

"It sounds great. But that part about staying until I get tired of you? If that's the yardstick he'll never see you again."

She grinned and walked over to me and knelt down in front of me. As she started licking my cock I said:

"Can I ask you a question?"

"Sure, ask away."

"What's your name?"

She grinned, "I wondered if you were ever going to ask. It's Debbie" and she went back to working on my cock.

~~~***~~~

Hitch Hiker Denise

I was leaning against the door of the car trying to catch a short nap. It was a Union 76 truck stop and I was parked in the back of the lot where it was fairly dark. On the way from Kansas City to Denver I had gotten sleepy and had caught myself nodding off and I figured I better pull over before I ran off the road and killed myself. I had been there about three hours and while I had gotten some sleep it had been a fitful nap what with air brakes hissing on and off. The whining of the diesel engines as the trucks pulled into and out of the lot didn't help either.

I had just made up my mind to go into the restaurant, drink a gallon of hot black coffee and hit the road when there was a 'tap tap' on the window. I sat up and looked out to see a young girl standing there. I rolled the window down and waited for her to tell me what she wanted. I'd heard about hookers who worked truck stops, but this girl looked way too young to be a hooker. It turned out that she both was and wasn't - it just depended on the way you looked at it.

"Mister, I haven't eaten in three days and I'm desperate. I'll give you a blow job for the price of a meal."

Obviously she wasn't a real hooker, not if she was giving blow jobs away for what amounted to less than ten bucks. I told her to get in the car and once she was in she looked at me nervously and said:

"I only done it once before, but I'll try real hard to do it good."

I started the car and I saw sudden panic on her face, "Relax, the first thing you need to learn about selling yourself is to get paid up front."

I drove the car up to the parking area by the restaurant and parked.

"Come on," I said, "Let's get you fed."

She started to order a typical kids meal, burger and fries, but I wouldn't let her; I ordered the top sirloin, baked potato and a trip to the all you can eat salad bar. She made two trips to the salad bar and it was the first chance I'd had to get a good look at her. Not a bad figure, at least as far as I could tell considering her baggy clothes, and a very pretty face all be it a slightly dirty one. After she had finished her meal I asked her how old she was and she told me she was eighteen and asked me why I wanted to know.

"Because you don't look old enough and guys can go to jail for messing with girls who aren't old enough."

She dug in her pocket and came out with a driver's license that she handed me. Her name was Denise and she had been eighteen for almost a week. It took some prying on my part, but I finally got her story out of her.

She left home on her eighteenth birthday and was heading for California where she hoped to find a girl friend of hers that had moved there. She didn't have much money when she left and what little she'd had ran out by the time she reached St. Louis. When I asked her why she hadn't waited until she had more money before making the trip she told me that she just couldn't wait any longer. It seems that her step father had been telling her when she reached eighteen he was going to make a woman out of her. Her mother had treated it as a joke, but Denise knew that he meant it. Denise had run away from home twice and both times her mother had called the police and they had found her and taken her back home. I asked her why she hadn't turned him in to the cops and she told me she was afraid to. I ordered apple pie ala mode for desert and then we went out and got in the car.

"Are we going to do it here? I'd rather go in the back where it's dark."

I smiled at her, "Sorry to disappoint you honey, but I'm not going to let you suck my dick. I just can't bring myself to take advantage of someone in trouble. You will have to pay for your dinner by keeping me company on my way to Denver and helping me stay awake. You got a bag or anything back there that you need?"

She didn't and I pulled out onto I-70 and headed for Denver.

About an hour down the road she slid over next to me and put her hand on my leg. I glanced over at her and saw that she was looking at me:

"I want to" she said.

"Not while I'm driving" I said, "We will be in Denver in seven hours and if you still want to when we get there maybe I'll let you."

Now, I love blow jobs as much as the next guy and this was the first time in my life that I had ever shied away from one, but something about this situation just didn't set right with me. I think it was because Denise was young enough to be my daughter, well almost. I was thirty-five and my daughter was fifteen.

But good intentions don't necessarily override a hard cock. When I told her no she stayed sitting beside me with her hand on my leg and after a few miles she fell asleep leaning against my shoulder and eventually she slid down and ended up with her head using my leg for a pillow. Unfortunately my cock just happened to be lying along my right leg only inches from her head and as she moved around trying to get comfortable she put her head on it and, quite naturally, it began to grow. As it grew she felt it grow and she raised her head up and looked at the lump developing and placed her hand on it and that was all it took.

I pulled over on the shoulder and unzipped and let Denise have her way. She might have only done it once before, but the girl had a natural talent for sucking cock and it only took her three minutes to get me to the point of cumming. I almost told her that I was going to shoot, but then I decided not to. She was going to have to learn to swallow sooner or later, especially if she was going to continue to pay for things with blow jobs. When the first spurt came out it caught her completely by surprise and she gagged and tried to pull her head up, but I held her in place and she was forced to gulp and swallow it all. When I was limp I let go of her head and she jerked it up and gave me a look that would kill.

"What's the matter?" I asked, "You don't understand that a blow job includes swallowing?"

Her anger changed to a sheepish look and she mumbled a no.

"Better get in the back seat to sleep. If you stay up here using my leg for a pillow we might never get to Denver."

* * *

She had expected me to let her out on I-70 when I reached my exit, but I kept on driving until we got to my house. I pulled in my driveway, shut off the car and said:

"We'll get you a shower, see if we can find you a change of clothes or two and then see what we can do about getting you on your way to California."

While she was in the shower I dug through the clothes that my ex-wife had left behind trying to find something that Denise could use. I finally gave up and figured that I would let Denise do the digging and let her pick out what she wanted. I was in the kitchen fixing breakfast when she came in wearing nothing but a bra and panties and I immediately noticed that her body was a lot better than I had suspected. I took her to the bedroom and showed her the stuff that Elise had left behind and told her to go through it and take what she wanted. Ten minutes later she came back wearing a dress and said, "How does this look?"

I told her that she looked great and that breakfast was ready. After breakfast was over with she went back to the bedroom and for the next hour she kept coming back and modeling things for me.

I was on the phone calling in a favor when I heard her say, "How's this?"

I turned and saw her in a pair of high heels and a black see through nightie. She did a little turn in front of me and said:

"What do you think?"

My response was the expected one and when she knelt down in front of me she said:

"Tell me this time, okay? I'll swallow; I just don't want to be surprised."

The favor I'd called in was a job for Denise. I told her she could stay with me, no strings attached, using my daughters old room until she had enough money to head for California. We went to the mall that afternoon and I got her all the things that women need, lipstick and other cosmetics, hair stuff, some underwear and socks and then I drove her over to see Andy. I'd talked him into hiring Denise as a receptionist/file clerk and she was to start the next day. I left the two of them to talk and ran a couple of errands and when I came back Andy was all smiles:

"She knows computers. I've been having all kinds of problems with my system and she has just about got it straightened out. I think you just helped make my life a little easier."

On the way back to the house Denise said, "He's nice. I think I'll like working for him."

I fixed us some dinner and then we watched TV for a while and around nine I told her that I was going to bed and I left her watching some game show. I was just stepping out of the shower when she walked in on me wearing the same heels and nightie that she had worn earlier in the day:

"They worked this morning so I thought I would try them again." She grinned at me; "It seems like it's having the desired effect."

I led her to the bed and she said, "This time I want you to do me, okay?"

I looked at her lying there so virginal and innocent looking and I almost didn't do it - almost! She was tight, extremely tight and from the faces she was making it seemed like I was hurting her and so I stopped and tried to pull away from her, but she grabbed me and said, "Don't stop, please, just do it."

I kept pushing and suddenly she gave a cry of pain and just as suddenly I knew what was going on - I had just taken her virginity. Well, there wasn't anything for it but to press on. When it was over she said:

"They tell me it gets better. Is that true? It wasn't really too bad there at the end."

I assured her that it did indeed get better.

"Can we do it again?"

It was a long night.

* * *

Denise never did sleep in the other bedroom. She spent her nights in my bed and she never did leave for California. For the first two months or so Denise wanted to fuck two or three times a night and she wanted to do everything. She loved having her pussy eaten, she loved fucking, she loved sucking my cock and she absolutely loved anal sex. I did my best to try and stay with her, but eventually she wore me down to where I was only able to go once a night for five or six days a week or twice a night for two or three nights a week. For all practical purposes we might as well have been married. We shared the cooking and cleaning, but I wouldn't let her pay any of the expenses so she saved up her money to buy a car.

She started dating fellows around her own age, staying out till midnight or two in the morning and then coming home and climbing into bed with me. She was always horny after a date and so she always woke me up to take care of her. Inevitably the night came when she came home and got me up and I discovered that I was not the first one to gain entry to her that night. She never said a word other than:

"Fuck me honey, fuck me. I need it bad."

The feel of my cock sliding into someone else's cum was not a new one for me, in fact that feeling was the reason that Elise and I were no longer married - I'd slid into her cum filled cunt one too many times. But I had no claim on Denise and she wasn't breaking any vows by spreading her legs for someone else.

Where it got touchy, at least for me, was the first time Denise came to me after someone else had fucked her and wanted me to eat her. She didn't ask, she just got into a sixty-nine with me. I could see that her pussy had already been serviced and I hesitated to put my mouth on her. She squirmed around trying to push her pussy down on my mouth and finally she whined:

"Please honey, please. You know how much I like it."

I gave in and began to lick and suck her cunt. After that once or twice a week Denise would come home from a date after having been fucked and want me to eat her. Soon it moved up to three or four times a week and since she didn't have a steady boyfriend I began to wonder if maybe some of Elise had remained on her clothes and had been transferred to Denise, turning her into just as big a slut as Elise had been. I didn't have to wonder about it for long.

I threw a card party one Friday night for a bunch of old friends. I had expected Denise to go out since she hardly ever stayed in on the weekend, but for some reason she stayed home that Friday night. For the first couple of hours she served as a hostess and raised a few eyebrows, you know, a jab in the ribs and "You and her? You old dog you" type comments.

About two and a half hours into the game Jerry got up to go to the bathroom and when he didn't come back in about ten minutes Glen got up to go and see what was keeping him. When neither of them were back in five minutes I got up to go and see what was happening. I found both of them in the bedroom buried in Denise. Glen had his cock in her mouth and Jerry had her legs up on his shoulders and was pounding away at her pussy. I heard "Damn!" from behind me and I turned to see that Ron and Dave had followed me and were looking over my shoulder.

The poker game was off and the gangbang was on.

It bothered me a little to see these thirty-five year old guys fucking that little eighteen year old girl, but then I thought, "You fucking hypocrite, you're thirty-five and you've been fucking her for six months now."

The gangbang lasted until two o'clock in the morning and as the guys were getting dressed they asked Denise if they could do it again some time. She surprised the hell out of me by pointing at me and saying:

"You will have to ask him. I will if he will let me."

I mumbled that I'd think about it and everyone left. I walked back to the bedroom and Denise was lying there waiting for me.

"Are you mad?"

I shrugged and said, "You don't belong to me. You are free to do what you want to."

Her face clouded up and she looked like she was going to cry.

"What did I say? Why are you going to cry?"

"I thought I meant something to you. I do belong to you and I thought you knew that."

"If you belong to me what about all the screwing you do during the week? You don't ask for my approval or permission to do that."

"That's different. I don't do it here and I always come home to you when I'm done."

Now there was pure logic for you. If Elise could have sold me on that we would still be married. Given her logic I just had to ask, "If that's so why didn't you ask me if you could do what you did tonight?"

"That was a fluke. I'm not used to having to lock the bathroom door and I was in there naked when Jerry walked in on me. It surprised us both and things just kind of happened and when Glen walked in on us it didn't seem like the time to quibble over things."

I was amazed at her reasoning process, but the bottom line was what was I going to do? On the one hand I liked having her around, but on the other she was doing everything that my ex-wife did that made me kick her ass out. The only difference was that Denise wasn't sneaking around and lying about it. However Denise looked at it (the 'I belong to you" remark) she was still an unencumbered free agent. The answer to the 'what was I going to do' question came easier than I thought. As I stood looking down at her and thinking she asked:

"You want me the way I am, or should I take a shower first?"

The answer?

I undressed and climbed into bed with her.

* * *

The Friday night poker game became a weekly event although precious little got done in the way of card playing. We held the group at seven, the maximum number for seven card stud, just in case we actually had to play cards (Denise's time of the month sometimes got in the way).

Denise still dated during the week, although not as much as she had, and on most of those nights I found myself sliding into a cum-filled cunt or eating it or both. Denise has a birthday coming up in a week and I asked her what she wanted for her birthday. You could have knocked me over with a feather when she said:

"I want you to marry me."

"Are you sure that's what you want? You will have to give up all your boyfriends and the Friday night poker game."

"Oh don't be silly. You know you like making love to me after somebody else has."

I'm taking her shopping for a ring tomorrow.

~~~***~~~

Hitch Hiker Joyce

My wife Joyce was a virgin when we married and I might as well have been one considering how little sexual experience I had. The novelty of sex itself kept us pretty occupied for the first couple of years. Most of our experimenting was along the lines of position changes - going from missionary to doggy style was a big thing for us. Thanksgiving dinner at my brother's house changed all that for us.

Thanksgiving dinner was a rotating family affair. One year my sister had the family over, then it was our turn and then the next year it was my brother Jeff's turn. Joyce's family was 1400 miles away so they didn't enter into the mix. Dinner at Jeff's was the same as dinner at everyone else's, depending on timing it was watch football and then eat dinner, eat and then watch football or watch football and eat at the same time. About halfway through the afternoon I began to notice that Joyce was a little on the nervous side. I also noticed that she was going to the bathroom almost once every hour and I started wondering if she was okay. After her fourth trip to the bathroom in as many hours I asked her if she was all right. She gave me an odd look, but said that she was fine.

It wasn't until we got home that night that I found out what had happened. Joyce had gone to use the bathroom and she noticed that there was a small magazine rack between the toilet and the vanity counter. She reached down and pulled out one of the magazines and started thumbing through it. It was a copy of Penthouse Letters and as she leafed through it she became curious and started reading some of the letters.

"You won't believe some of the stuff I read" and she took it out of her purse and handed it to me. She had kept on going back to the bathroom so she could read more of the magazine and she finally ended up sneaking into her purse and bringing it home with her. "Turn to page twelve" she said, I did and so began our journey toward sexual discovery.

I know it is going to sound like we were very naïve (and we were) but even though I ate Joyce's pussy a lot (she loved it) and she sucked my cock a lot (I loved it) we had never even thought of doing it at the same time. Page twelve changed that. The letters on page twelve and succeeding pages were all on oral sex and after reading the letters we tried sixty-nine for the very first time and we both loved it. The next night we tried something from another letter - I ate Joyce after I'd made love to her - my very first cream pie. There were plenty of other letters and we got hot reading them and then we fucked like horny teenagers.

* * *

The following Monday when I got home from work Joyce said, "Guess what I did today? I went out and got the new issue of Penthouse Letters and I sent in the little card to get a subscription."

From the point on PHL became our sexual road map. We would read the letters, get new ideas and then put them into practice. We tried anal sex for the first time and after the initial discomfort Joyce found that she loved it. We had sex in public places where the chance of getting discovered existed and we tried role-playing and had a lot of fun. But the letters that turned on Joyce the most were the ones where men watched their wives and the ones where a wife would have sex with a black man. I didn't really know how I felt about either of those two, but it didn't matter because they were only fantasies. It was obvious that the letters covering those subjects were Joyce's favorites because when she read them she became insatiable. For four or five days after reading an issue with either or both of those topics she couldn't keep her hands off of me. Just out of curiosity, one day I asked her if she ever planned on trying either of them for real.

"Don't be silly. The idea turns me on, but no way could I ever become that big of a slut."

The next several years went by and, thanks to PHL and magazines like it, our sex life hummed right along. Even though Joyce and I never discussed her two favorite fantasies in detail, at least as far as actually doing them, we did act them out in the bedroom.

* * *

Because Joyce's family lived 1400 miles away we spent one week of vacation with them a year and we went to see them every other Christmas. It was summer vacation and we were on our way to visit them. We were headed east on I-70 and it was raining buckets. We saw a figure up ahead walking along the Interstate, shoulders hunched down against the driving rain, not even trying to thumb a ride. In this day and age hardly anyone will pick up a hitchhiker and whoever it was on the side of the road had probably given up trying. Normally I don't pick up hikers either, but it was raining hard and it was at least twenty-five miles to the next exit so I stopped and told him to get in the back.

He was a young black man and he said he was on his way to Hayes, Kansas when his car broke down. We were an hour and a half from Hayes so I told him I could take him all the way. He thanked me and then leaned back against the seat and closed his eyes. For the next ten minutes it was very quiet in the car except for the sound of the windshield wipers and tire noise. Joyce kept glancing into the back seat and then back at me. Finally she said, "He doesn't know us and we will never see him again" and before her words had a chance to register on me she turned and climbed over the seat into the back. I took my foot off the gas and was about to hit the brakes when Joyce said:

"Please honey, just keep driving please?"

I looked in the rear view to see that she had already taken off her sweatshirt (she usually goes bra-less on trips) and had pulled the man's mouth to her tits. No way I can stop her now, I thought, at least not without doing major damage to our relationship. The possibility that her actions might just have done the damage was something I wouldn't know till it was over and we had a chance to talk. I wasn't too sure that I was going to be happy about what was taking place. When it was a fantasy it was one thing, but now?

I adjusted the rear view mirror so I could keep an eye on things and went back to driving. I kept glancing into the rear view and then back at the road so I missed a lot, but I saw enough to realize that what Joyce was doing was turning me on. The man had one of her tits in his mouth and he was squeezing the other one as Joyce's hands were busy trying to get his cock out of his pants. As soon as she had it free she started to jack him off. The man ran a hand down inside Joyce's sweatpants and she moaned as his fingers found her opening. For a couple of minutes she stroked his cock while he sucked her tits and finger fucked her and then she suddenly pulled away from him, pushed off her sweats and panties and straddled the man. I couldn't see from my angle, but I heard her sudden intake of breath when the man's cock split her pussy lips and went into her cunt. For the next ten or twelve miles all I could see was Joyce's back as she rode up and down on the black man's cock, but I could hear her as she moaned:

"Yes, yes, oh yes, oh god yes, fuck me, fuck me."

Finally I heard the man gasp "I'm gonna cum lady, I'm gonna cum."

I expected Joyce to get off of him and finish him by hand, but she stayed where she was and moaned:

"Give it to me, give it to me, give it to me."

I hoped to god she had her diaphragm in because I know she hadn't put a rubber on him. Joyce climbed off the man and she looked into the mirror and into my eyes:

"I'm sorry honey. I don't know what came over me, but all of a sudden I just had to do it."

There wasn't a whole lot I could say to that, but what I was going to say was, "Get back up here and take care of me now" because my cock was as hard as a rock. However, before I could say that I noticed her hand move over to the black man's limp dick and start to fondle it and after a minute or so it began to grow again. Between watching the road and watching the mirror I missed the transition, but all of a sudden she had her head in the man's lap, he had his hands on the back of her head and was fucking Joyce's mouth. Another fifteen miles and I heard him say, "Here it comes, here it comes" and I saw him arch up and I knew that my wife had just taken a mouthful of cum. She kept her mouth on him and in another five miles it was hard enough again to suit her. She lay back on the seat, spread her legs and the man moved between them. For the next thirty miles I watched a black ass with white hands on it move up and down while Joyce moaned with pleasure and begged him not to stop. For the third time since we picked him up I heard him say he was going to cum and again I heard Joyce say, "Give it to me, give it to me." The man gave a grunt and fell forward on top of Joyce and she wrapped her arms around him and pulled him to her.

* * *

She was sitting next to the man, stroking his cock, as I rolled past the Hayes city limit sign.

"Where would you like me to let you off" I asked.

He grinned, "I've never in my life had a ride like this one and I would like to show my thanks. If you'll take me to my house I'll have you in for dinner. That way you won't have to stop at a restaurant."

I saw in the mirror that Joyce's hand had his cock erect again and I was all set to say no thanks when Joyce said:

"We would like that, wouldn't we honey."

I knew damned well if I stopped at that house that the only thing that was going to get fed was Joyce's pussy so I said:

"We are running way behind sweetie and I think we should keep moving."

Joyce, in a very pleading tone of voice said, "Please honey, do it for me, please?"

I was right! We were no sooner in the house than the two of them were tearing off clothes. The black man (we still didn't know his name) sat down on the couch and Joyce knelt between his legs and started sucking his cock. After several minutes she stopped sucking his cock and climbed on top of him and sat on his dick. For the first time I actually got to see his dark pole slide into her white body and I have to admit that it was one of the most erotic things I'd ever seen. I'd had a hard on since Joyce had climbed into the back seat and it had been my intention to pull over to the side of the road after we dropped off the man and fuck Joyce myself.

Watching that black cock sliding into her had me thinking that I was going to have to pull my cock out and start beating it and I was reaching for my zipper when the front door opened and a black man and black woman walked in. They stopped dead in their tracks at the sight of what was going on in front of them and then the woman said, "For Christ's sake Norman, at least have the decency to take her into the bedroom. I don't want stains all over my couch."

The sound of her voice caused Joyce to turn around and her hands automatically went to cover her tits. The woman laughed:

"Don't bother honey. You're not the first one of Norman's sluts that I've seen."

Joyce looked a little on the embarrassed side as she and Norman got off the couch and Norman led her toward the back of the house. The woman looked at me:

"You going with them?"

I shook my head no.

"You her pimp?"

Again I shook my head no and said, "I'm her husband."

She gave me an odd look, "You do this often? Take her to fuck other men?"

I gave her a rueful smile, "No. This is the first time" and I explained Joyce's fantasy and how we had picked up Norman and what had happened since. While I was talking to the woman the black man who had come in with her walked to the back of the house. He came back after a couple of minutes and sat down in an easy chair. He turned on the TV, but it couldn't hold his interest and he kept looking toward the back of the house. The woman said:

"Is this going to be the only time, or are you going to let her make a habit of it?"

It was an interesting question and I told her that I had no idea where this episode was going to take us. She noticed the man on the easy chair looking toward the back of the house and finally said:

"For God's sake Harold, just go!"

He was out of the chair like a horse out of the starting gate and heading for the back of the house. The woman said:

"I don't know what it is about black men and white pussy. It must be something that is hard wired into their brains. She ever had two men at the same time before?"

I shook my head no and she said, "Well, we better keep them two away from the phone or we will end up with half the black dicks in the neighborhood in here and it might be days before you can get back on the road. By the way, I'm Jolene" and she offered me her hand. I introduced myself and she said, "You want to stay here and talk to me or would you rather go see what your wife looks like with two dicks to play with?"

Actually I did want to go and see, but this woman and her matter of fact attitude toward her husband/boyfriend/brother (whatever) fucking my wife intrigued me.

"I'll stay with you, at least for a while."

She laughed, "You wondering what dark meat is like? You going to try and get your dick in me?"

I told her no (and I thought I detected a little disappointment in her eyes when I said it) and that I was just curious about her attitude toward what was going on in the bedroom.

"Do you let him do things like that very often?"

She laughed, "No sugar, normally I'd scratch the eyes out of any slut I caught even looking at Harold, but not this time. She's white and I know that black men have a huge curiosity about what they are like. As long as she is here and is fucking Norman I'll let Harold satisfy his curiosity."

"How about you" I asked, "You curious about white men?"

She laughed, "Oh you smoothie. You do want a piece of my black ass, don't you?"

I'm sure that I blushed, "No, I'm just curious about whether the black white thing holds for the women also."

"I don't think so" she said, "Most of the women I know get pissed when they see their menfolk look at white women, but I don't see them trying out white men. How about white men? Are they like white women in their desire to try out a little black meat?"

I had to think about that for a moment or two.

"I don't think so. Most guys I know just want pussy and they don't seem to care if it is white, black, red, yellow or even green."

"Well sugar, I've never really thought about doing a white man, but you are here and if I know Harold and Norman as well as I think I do you are going to be here for quite a while so I might as well see what you got."

If I had any choice in the matter it was gone when she reached over and felt the lump in my trousers. I said:

"You know that after all that I've watched that I'm going to cum pretty quick."

She giggled, "I can take care of that sugar. Trust me on that."

She took me by the hand and led me toward the back of the house and past the bedroom where Norman and Harold were fucking Joyce and I stopped for a moment to watch. Joyce was sitting on Harold's cock and she was bent forward so Norman could stuff his cock up her ass. Her tits were swinging from side to side and she was moaning, "Oh fuck oh fuck oh fuck oh god yes" as the two cocks moved in and out of her.

Jolene gave me a tug and led me into the back bedroom. She sucked my cock and I came almost immediately (I was a gentleman - I told her it was on the way), but she kept my dick in her mouth until I was hard again and then she fucked me. Then she asked me if I would mind eating her pussy:

"I got to warn you - I fucked Harold before we went to the store and I haven't cleaned myself yet."

I grinned and dove right in and listened to her squeal as I sucked her pussy. She twisted around and went into a sixty-nine with me until she got me hard again and then she straddled me and fucked me. We had just finished when we heard Joyce cry out and then the cry was choked off. Jolene giggled:

"Sounds like the white slut just had a cock stuck in her mouth."

We got up and walked to the other bedroom and looked in.

"I told you we needed to keep them away from the phone."

There were five men in the room and the reason for Joyce's cry was obvious - the black man working his cock into her ass had the biggest cock I had ever seen.

"Oh my" Jolene said, "I never realized that Ozzie was so well equipped. Maybe I shouldn't have slapped his face the last time he made a pass at me."

She giggled and said, "If he ever does it again… oh fuck, come on sugar, you're not going to get her out of here any time soon. We may as well join the party."

She led me over to the bed, pushed me down next to the three guys and my wife and climbed on top of me. Joyce saw me out of the corner of her eye, but never took her mouth off of the cock in it to say anything. I did think I saw disapproval in her eyes, but if that's what it was I ignored it. The rest of the night was pure orgy as all six of us guys took turns on the two women. I did have to smile at the pissed off expression on Harold's face as he watched Ozzie slide his huge cock into Jolene and the look on Jolene's face told me that it was something that was going to happen again and again - whether Harold liked it or not.

* * *

It was eight in the morning before we were ready to hit the road again. Jolene had offered to fix breakfast for us, but I knew that if we sat down and took the time to fix breakfast and then eat it the orgy would start up all over again. Norman asked us to stop back on the way home and I saw from the look in Joyce's eyes that she was going to work on me to do just that. Jolene walked us to the car and as Joyce was getting in on the passenger side Jolene kissed me.

"Hey white boy, I don't want to scare you, but if you stop here again you might never get that slut of yours back home. What happened here last night will be known by every black cock in this town by noon today. If you come back God alone only knows how many she'll have to take on. God knows that after last night I'm going to be fighting them off for a long time to come."

"That's her problem" I said, "She started it and I know she's going to work on me to stop on the way back. Just you make sure that Ozzie leaves enough for me, okay?"

She giggled, "You noticed? I hope Harold didn't."

She kissed me again and I got in the car.

"What was that all about" Joyce wanted to know.

"Nothing. Just wanted to know if I was going to bring you back."

"What did you tell her?"

I turned to her, "You and I have an awful lot of talking to do in the next eleven hundred miles."

~~~***~~~

Hitch Hiker Lee Ann

I was parked in the back row at the Little America truck stop when someone started beating on the passenger door of my rig. I had just climbed up into the sleeper and zipped the curtain so it took me a second or two to get up, open the curtain and look out and the whole time the beating continued. The parking lot was full of flashing red and blue lights and I wondered just what the fuck was going on. Someone was still pounding on the door so I leaned over to see who it was and got a bit of a shock when I saw it was Lee Ann. What the hell was she doing here? The last time I saw her she was in Colorado. I reached over and lowered the window, "What do you want?"

"I need help."

"You need help and you come to me?"

"All right, so you hate my guts, but it won't kill you to give me a break here."

"Where's your boy Brandon?"

"He split about five minutes ago. Now either let me in your truck or tell me to fuck off, but do something."

I reached over and popped the door lock and told her to get in.

"What's happening?"

"The cops raided the place and they are rounding up all the hookers."

"And your main squeeze took off and abandoned you? You sure can pick 'em kid."

She didn't look at me or respond so I said, "Get up in the sleeper and get your clothes off." She gave me a nasty look and I said, "You wish. I wouldn't touch you with Brandon's dick. If you want me to save your worthless ass get in the sleeper and get your fucking clothes off. You have to look like you belong here."

She gave me a dirty look, but then she climbed up into the sleeper and I followed her in. I watched her strip and thought, not for the first time, that she had the most fantastic and fuckable body that I had ever seen. Her eyes locked onto mine and never left as she took off her clothes. Once she was naked she cupped her hands around her 36D's and tweaked the nipples and despite my efforts to hold it down my dick started to respond. Lee Ann noticed and gave me what I can only call a smirk. I was about to call her a bitch when someone started pounding on the door of the truck. I waited and made them bang again and then I stuck my head out of the curtain and yelled, "Who is it?"

"Police! Open up!"

"Just a minute. I need to put my pants on."

I pulled on my jeans, climbed out of the sleeper, rolled down the window and looked down to see two cops - one fat and one skinny.

"What's this all about?"

The fat one said, "We want the woman who just climbed up into your truck. Send her out."

"Why?"

"Don't get smart asshole. You know damned well why."

"Asshole? You calling me an asshole? Listen you fat tub of guts, I asked you a question and you can either give me an answer or you can fuck off."

"Okay wise guy. You want to play it that way we can. You got a hooker in there with you and we are going to haul her off to jail. You, smart mouth, will get a half a dozen tickets as soon as you pull your rig off this lot."

"You're calling my wife a hooker? Have you been sued lately for slander? Is that what you're fishing for?"

"Don't give that 'your wife' shit. We saw here climb up in your cab as soon as we pulled onto the lot. Now put her out."

"You got a supervisor here? Somebody in charge?"

"Why?"

"Go and get him. Ain't nothing going to happen here until I talk to him and then, depending on his attitude, I may or may not press charges against you."

He told the skinny cop to stay and keep an eye on me, "Make sure the bitch doesn't get out and slip away."

He came back about five minutes later with a cop who had sergeant stripes on his sleeve. He cut right to the chase:

"Officer Mace says you are giving him problems."

"No, it's the other way around. The officer beat on my door, woke me up, started calling me an asshole and my wife a hooker and then he told me that he didn't like my attitude and that my attitude had just earned me a half a dozen tickets."

The fat cop said, "He's lying sarge. You know I don't talk to citizens like that."

The sergeant said, "I'm sorry sir, but I'll have to ask you and the woman to step down out of the truck."

I said, "Okay, but first I have to bring you up to speed about your lying officer. I have been driving trucks for a living for over twenty years now and if there is one thing I have learned the hard way it's that there are police who don't like truckers and who go out of their way to cause them trouble and stick them with tickets. I've learned to cover myself when they are around."

I reached behind me and picked up the cassette recorder that I'd started when I climbed out of the sleeper and hit the play button. I watched the blood drain from the fat cop's face as the sergeant listened to every word that fat cop had said.

"He probably did see my wife climb up in the cab, but that was because she had just come back from using the restroom in the restaurant."

I opened up my briefcase and got out my fuel slip and handed it down to him.

"You can see what time I pulled in here for fuel."

I hollered back to the sleeper, "Lee Ann, hand me out your driver's license" and a moment later she passed it out to me. I took out mine and handed them both to the sergeant and called back to Lee Ann to stick her head out so the sergeant could match her face to the license.

"You will notice the last names and addresses are the same. Something your officer could have verified in less time than it took him to go and get you if he had behaved the way that the public expects the police to behave."

The sergeant handed me back the stuff I had given him. "I'm sorry for the inconvenience and rest assured that Officer Mace and I will have a very long and not so nice talk about this" and the three cops left.

I gave Lee Ann back her license and she said, "Thanks for lying for me."

"It was only half a lie. The divorce isn't final yet so technically you are still my wife. As for the other part, you are a whore, but not a hooker. At least you didn't used to charge for it."

"Well, that has changed. Brandon has been charging guys so I guess that makes him a pimp and me a prostitute."

We were interrupted by the sergeant who had come back. "I know it's not fair, but I would suggest you leave now. Mace will tell the others how you burned him and they will find a way to nail you when you leave. Which way you headed?"

"North, to Bozeman."

"Well, I'll keep everybody busy here until you have had time to get out of our jurisdiction, but I'd be real careful coming through here from now on. I'd also hang on to that tape. It might prove useful if Mace or one of his buddies ever gets you into court."

I thanked the man, got dressed and fired up the diesel. Lee Ann said, "What are you doing?"

"I'm doing what the man said I ought to do, I'm getting the hell out of here."

"But what about me?"

"Unfortunately, for me anyway, you just became a hitch hiker. If you get out now they will know I lied and they would probably throw both of our asses in jail. You're stuck with me until I can find a way to reunite you with your pimp."

As I pulled through the lot I saw that the sergeant had probably been right. I got several nasty looks from the cops and saw a couple writing down my rig and plate numbers. I pulled out of the lot and headed north on the Interstate. The first exit I came to I got off, crossed the overpass and got on the southbound side. Lee Ann asked, "Why did you do that?"

"Because I don't trust cops. I told him I was going north to throw him off. I'll bet there are at least two county mounties waiting for me on the northbound side. For all I know he might have called ahead and got this side covered too. We'll find out pretty soon."

"But why? Why would he do something like that?"

"Because he's a cop and they all stick together."

Neither of us said another word from there to the Colorado state line.

A little background here; Lee Ann and I had been married up until four months ago. Technically we were still married because the divorce wasn't final yet. The first three years of our marriage Lee Ann used to travel with me as co-driver, but eventually the novelty wore off and she started staying home. The next three years went by and I thought we had a good marriage and then one day as I was pulling out of the yard for a trip to Kansas City my tranny locked up. No other truck was available so I went on home. I walked in the front door just in time to hear Lee Ann cry out, "Oh Jesus oh god yes, like that, just like that, fuck me baby fuck me."

My heart turned to stone and my feet felt they were in buckets of cement as I walked toward the bedroom. The sounds of Lee Ann and whoever was there with her were hitting my ears like someone beating on me with boxing gloves. I reached the bedroom door and looked in; I recognized the man right away - it was my brother Brandon. Lee Ann was on her knees with her butt stuck up in the air and Brandon was pounding into her from behind and, if I wasn't mistaken, he was pounding into her behind. They were both facing away from me and neither one of them noticed me.

I stood there for two or three more minutes, watching and listening to the two of them and then I reached over and flicked the light switch a couple of times. They both turned to see me standing there and it was almost comical to see the two of them trying to get away from each other. Lee Ann started to say something, but I held up my hand:

"I'm the only one who has something to say here. I'm leaving for an hour and when I come back I'm going to hurt anyone who is still here. I'll make that two hours - just to give you enough time to get all your stuff out of here. I don't want you to have to come back for anything. I don't ever want to set eyes on either one of you again."

I turned to leave and Lee Ann cried out, "Wait! Let me explain" but I kept walking and when I got to the front door I turned and hollered, "Two hours; two hours and not one fucking minute more!"

I called a locksmith and made an appointment to meet him at the house in three hours and then I went and found a bar. When I came back Lee Ann and all of her stuff was gone. Lee Ann called several times, but I always hung up on her and I hadn't seen her again until tonight.

We had just crossed the state line when Lee Ann said, "Why wouldn't you ever talk to me?"

"Because you didn't have anything to say that I needed to hear. There wasn't any way you were going to convince me that what I saw was a figment of my imagination so what else was there?"

"You could have at least let me explain why."

"Why? What difference would that have made? You really think you could have told me why and that I would have said "Oh, that's okay if that's why you did it." It wouldn't have changed a fucking thing."

"No, but you might have been a little nicer, a little more understanding if you were to understand that you were part of the cause."

I laughed and said, "Somehow I just knew that it was going to turn out to be my fault."

"Not all yours, but you had a hand in it. Oh, the major blame is mine and I'll accept seventy-five percent of it. Brandon gets maybe ten percent, but you get the rest."

"Go ahead, I just have to hear how it was my fault."

"You are the one who got me to liking sex. The first three years of our marriage you were after me damn near every night. When I stopped riding with you the sex stopped too. You would be gone on a nine day trip, come home for three days and then be gone for another seven or nine days. I was getting sex six or seven times a month instead of six or seven times a week and that just wasn't enough. I tried to talk you in to taking a regular job and staying home, but oh no, you just had to keep on trucking because you liked the freedom of the open road. Well, you might have had your freedom, but I was stuck at home with nothing but a rubber dildo for company. For almost two years I used nothing but that damned rubber dick even though what I really wanted was the real thing. I had plenty of opportunities to run around on you, but I passed them up because I loved you.

"Your parent's anniversary party changed all that. You were on the road again and so I had to go alone. I drank too much and your parents wouldn't let me drive; they made Brandon drive me home. I don't remember what happened after I got in the car, but when I woke up the next morning there was a naked man in bed with me. I thought you must have come home during the night and I slid down to wake you up with a blow job and when you were nice and hard I climbed up and slid down on your cock. The cock had just entered me when I saw that it wasn't you, it was Brandon. I started to get back off of him, but he grabbed me and held me there. I should have screamed and hollered and fought to get away, but I didn't. It felt so good to have a real cock in me instead of a rubber one that I just stayed there. Besides, it was obvious, given the fact that he was naked and in bed with me that he had fucked me the night before.

"After that every time you went out of town we fucked. It had nothing to do with my loving you, it was just sex and after a while it just didn't seem to matter. I took care of you when you were home, tried to keep you happy and I kept trying to get you to take a regular job. If you would have taken a job that would have kept you home I would have dropped Brandon in a heartbeat. When you were around you were all I really wanted, but you were gone more often than not. Not that you give a shit, but I don't even like your brother."

"Then why are you still with him?"

"Where was I supposed to go? I believed you when you said be gone or get hurt when you came back. I had no money and no place to go and Brandon said I could stay with him. I got a job flipping burgers and I intended to leave Brandon as soon as I saved enough for a place of my own. You have any idea how hard it is to save money on what you make flipping burgers?"

"How did you end up going from burger flipping to fucking for money?"

"The same way I ended up fucking Brandon. I got drunk one night and woke up the next morning with a friend of Brandon's lying in bed next to me. I guess he and Brandon had taken turns on me most of the night. When he left he told Brandon that I was worth every penny and when I asked what he meant Brandon told me that the guy had paid him to fuck me. After that, any time Brandon needed money he would get me drunk and sell me to someone, and Brandon always needed money. He sells drugs and he never seems to have enough to pay his supplier. Tonight was a perfect example. We had driven up to get five pounds of grass and he was a hundred dollars short so he took me to the truck stop and sold me to a couple of truckers. He didn't take the time to get me drunk this time and I basically got raped. Once he got the money he went and got the dope.

We stopped back at the truck stop for gas and I saw you at the fuel pumps so I ducked into the bathroom so you wouldn't see me. When I came out I saw you pulling around back to park. Brandon and I went into the restaurant to eat and then I used the bathroom again. When I came out

I saw the flashing lights and Brandon pulling out of the lot. He must have panicked and thought they might catch him with the grass. As a woman alone and with no car I knew I was going to be picked up with the rest of the hookers so I swallowed my pride and came to you for help."

We were both silent for the next fifteen or twenty miles and then she said, "I miss you. You will never know how sorry I am for what happened."

Well, the truth was that I missed her too. And she was right - I had left her home a lot, but damn it - I went without sex while I was gone. Was it too much to have expected her to do the same? Another ten miles of silence and then she said:

"Did you really mean it when you said you wouldn't touch me? I saw you looking at my naked breasts and I know you had a hard on."

"Yeah, well, you always could do that to me."

She took off her blouse and pushed down her bra, "Am I doing it now?"

It was too much for me. I hadn't been laid since I kicked her out and the truth of the matter was that I hadn't gone one single night since she left without thinking about her. I started down shifting and she knew right away what that meant. She scrambled up into the sleeper and started taking off her clothes:

"Hurry baby, hurry. I want you so bad."

As I pulled off on the shoulder and turned on my blinkers I wondered where this was going to take us. Well, if it took us back home together I guess that wouldn't be all bad.

~~~***~~~

Hitch Hiker Stephanie

It had been a long haul from New York to Detroit and as I was putting gas in the tank I was debating on whether to get another couple of hundred miles under my belt or find a motel and sack out. My thoughts were interrupted by a voice from behind me, "Excuse me sir" and I turned around to see a very attractive lady standing behind me.

"I noticed the Colorado plates on your car and I wondered if you were going to or coming from."

"Going to, I'm happy to say" I replied.

"Would you like some company? It can be a long drive for someone alone."

"Company would be nice, but I have a rule against hitch hikers ever since one of them robbed my brother."

"Do I look like a robber?"

"The girl that robbed him didn't look like one either."

"Can I buy you a cup of coffee and at least talk to you about it?"

Why not I thought, she was a damned good looking woman and I wouldn't mind staring at her over a cup of coffee. At the table she opened up her purse and took out a wad of cash big enough to choke a horse and said, "See? I don't need to rob you." I just looked at her and she returned the look and said, "Oh, I see. You think I got it from guys like you who gave me rides."

I shrugged and didn't say anything. "Okay" she said, "How about this? You put your cash and credit cards in an envelope and mail them to your home address and I'll pay the expenses until we get there."

It was a tempting offer; she would be good company if for no other reason than to look at, but I was still leery.

"Honey, I hate to sound paranoid, but what's to stop you from trying to blackmail me once we get there? You know, give me a thousand bucks or I'll tell the cops you raped me."

The look on her face said "Boy, you sure are some piece of work," but she didn't say anything, just got a pen and a piece of paper out of her purse. "What's your name?" I told her and she started writing. She handed the paper to me, "I, Stephanie Ann Gambellino, plan of my own free will on sucking the cock of (my name) every chance I get on the trip to Denver. I also, of my own free will plan on fucking him every chance I get."

She had signed it. I looked at her and she handed me her driver's license; sure enough, she was Stephanie Ann.

"Put that in the envelope and mail it with your other stuff."

"You sure must want to ride with me pretty bad. Want to tell me why?"

"You are on your way to Colorado and I need to get to Denver."

"Okay, but why not a train, plane or bus? You obviously can afford it."

"Can we just say that I have what I think are good reasons and let it go at that?"

"Okay Stephanie Ann, finish your coffee and let's get the show on the road. I want to get another hundred miles in before I stop for the night."

We didn't make a hundred miles. We didn't even make fifty. Five minutes onto I-94 she slid over next to me and her hand went to my zipper.

"What are you doing?"

She laughed and said, "Just what I said I was going to do - suck your cock every chance I get until we reach Denver."

I started looking for an exit with a motel, but it was another ten miles and by then she had me ready to blow. I told her I was going to cum and told her there were tissues in the glove box, but she didn't stop and I had to pull over until she finished.

"All the way to Denver huh?"

"All the way baby. If you can keep getting it up it might take us a while to get there."

"If you keep trying to get it up I know it will."

I pulled in at a Best Western and registered and we were barely inside the door to the room and she was trying to get my pants off me.

"Let me get it hard again baby and then we can take time to get naked."

She was a great cocksucker. She deep-throated me and I'll swear that I felt the head of my dick touch the back of her throat. When I was hard again I pushed her back on the bed, "My turn" I said as I buried my face in her muff. I like to eat pussy and I've been told that I'm pretty good at it and Stephanie seemed to enjoy it so I was a bit surprised when she pushed me away from her.

"I want you in me. Please, fuck me now. I need your cock in me."

She was hot, she was wet, but God was she tight. As wet and ready as she was it still took me about eight strokes to work my way in. She was a wild woman in bed; she kicked and screamed, bucked and twisted and had several orgasms before I had mine. As soon as I came she pushed me away from her and went down on me. She fought a losing battle to keep me from going soft and when that fact became obvious to her she stopped and said:

"Damn it, I'm still horny."

I grinned at her, "It will be back and I think I can keep you happy until it does" and I buried my face in her wet bush and went to work. It was a long night, but I didn't mind at all and I don't think she did either.

* * *

The next day, following breakfast, we headed on down the road. Two hours later I saw a sign telling me that there was a rest area half a mile ahead and she must have read my mind because she said, "Yeah! Park away from everyone else" and she climbed over the seat and laid down on the back seat. I drove that half-mile watching in the rear view mirror while she finger fucked herself. I pulled into the rest area and parked as far away from the other vehicles there as I could and then I joined Stephanie in the back seat. It was a no frills fuck that lasted almost twenty minutes and then we got back on the Interstate. Forty-five minutes later she slid over next to me and started playing with my cock.

We stopped three times that day and I didn't even cover three hundred miles. At that rate it was going to take me a week to get home, but I didn't care. Getting home would mean giving up this fantastic sex-crazy woman and I wanted to stall that as long as possible. Except for when she was trying to get my cock out of my pants Stephanie was quiet when we were driving; mostly she just stared out the window at the scenery lost in thought. I tried to find out something about her, but she avoided all conversation so eventually I stopped trying. We stopped for dinner and suddenly, in mid bite, she put her fork down and said:

"I'm running away."

I looked up from my plate and she said again, "I'm running away. That's what you wanted to know, isn't it?"

I put my fork down and took a sip of my iced tea, "Well, I do have to admit to a certain amount of curiosity when a gorgeous woman with a purse full of cash, who just happens to be a nymphomaniac, comes up to me and asks for a ride. Especially when she has the money to get there a whole lot quicker and in a little more comfort."

She laughed and said, "But I couldn't do what we've been doing on the plane, train or bus. You want to drop me off at an airport? Or would you rather have me, emphasis on the have, all the way to Denver?"

I threw up my hands and said, "Okay, okay, have it your way. What are you running away from?"

She looked down at her plate and pushed her mashed potatoes around with a fork:

"From an abusive husband."

I already knew enough not to go there so I asked, "Where in Denver are you going?"

"It's not really in Denver. It's a suburb of Denver called Castle Rock."

"Where in Castle Rock?"

"A place called the Woodlands."

"Where in the Woodlands?"

"On Pinyon, why?"

"Because I live in Castle Rock."

"My sister lives there. I haven't spoken to her in over eight years. She doesn't even know I'm coming. I just hope she can put me up for a few days until I can figure out what to do next."

"Can I ask why you haven't talked to her in eight years? Hell, I don't get along all that well with my sister, but we still talk on the phone two or three times a month."

"My father was dead set against her getting married and they had a big argument. I sided with my dad and she hasn't spoken to either of us since."

"Why didn't you go and stay with your dad?"

"Because that's the first place Rocco will go looking for me. He knows about my sister not having anything to do with me so he'll never think to look there."

That night was a repeat of the previous night and the next day was a carbon copy of the previous day. At the rate we were going it was going to take me five days to make a trip I usually made in twenty-three hours. Stephanie was usually quiet when we were driving, but she opened up when we stopped for meals and I found out a lot more about her. The reason her father had been against her sister's marriage was because he was sure, or was pretty sure that he knew, that the man she was marrying was hooked into organized crime.

"What is so ironic is that my dad pushed me into marrying my husband because he was good looking and had money. What he didn't know until it was too late was that my husband's money comes from the rackets. Ain't that a kick in the ass."

"Did you ever find out about your sisters husband?"

"No, she hasn't spoken one word to us since."

"How do you know she won't just slam the door in your face?"

"I don't know that she won't. I'm just hoping for the best."

"What happens if she does let you stay and your husband plays the long shot and finds you there?"

It's not likely. He will be spending most of his time looking for me in New York, but if he does find me I'll just split for someplace else."

"Why New York?"

"Before finding you I went out to Detroit Metropolitan Airport and found a sympathetic lady who let me buy her ticket in my name. When Rocco uses his contacts to check things he will find that my credit card bought a ticket to New York. I have some cousins there so that is where he will go."

"Why are you so sure that he will look for you?"

"Because to him I am a possession. And in the world he moves around in he will suffer a great loss of face because I took off."

That night she told me that she wanted to try something different, "You haven't had my ass yet and I love it up my ass."

* * *

We didn't get out of the motel until almost noon the next day and then we stopped at a rest area around two where she gave me one of her stupendous blow jobs. At six we were in the back seat of the car in a Union 76 truck stop parked way out on the back of the lot. We were ten hours from Denver and could have made it there by six in the morning, but she wanted one last night so we hit a motel. She damn near destroyed me that night; she managed to get me up five times and I was so whipped when the seven o'clock wake-up call came that I couldn't get out of bed. It was ten before we got on the road again.

For the first hour or so Stephanie was very quiet and then she said, "You live in Castle Rock, right?"

I nodded a yes.

"Any chance that I could stay with you if Rosalie does slam the door in my face?"

My eyebrows went up at that but I was quiet for a bit and then said, "It might be difficult, but maybe I can talk my wife into it."

"Oh Jesus, I never asked, did I? I never gave a thought to the fact that you might be married."

For the next ten minutes she stared out the window and then, "What kind of relationship do you have with your wife that she might let you talk her into letting me stay with you?"

I grinned and then said, "She needs more cock than I can give her, kind of like you in a way, so I let her go out and play. It keeps her happy and she, in turn, keeps me happy. The thing is I don't play around on her so you will be somewhat of a surprise and I don't know how she will take to sharing me. And she will have to share if you stay with us because I won't be able to keep my hands off of you."

She laughed and said, "You might not be able to get your hands on me. Your wife sounds like my kind of girl. If I stay with you I might just be going out with her to play."

I smiled at her, "I wouldn't be the least bit surprised."

After two stops on the road to satisfy Stephanie's urges we rolled into Castle Rock around nine in the evening. As I turned off Hwy 86 onto Woodlands Blvd Stephanie asked me where I was going.

"To Pinyon. All I need is an address."

She dug in her purse to find the number and told me what it was. I pulled into the driveway at the address and got Stephanie's small bag from the back seat,

"Come on honey, I'll be your moral support" and I walked her to the front door. She took a deep breath and pushed the doorbell and waited. No one came so she pressed it again. I waited about thirty seconds and then I reached past her and turned the door knob:

"I forgot. The bell doesn't work."

I pushed the door open and hollered "Rosalie, I'm home and have I got a surprise for you."

I stepped back and smiled at Stephanie, "After you sweetie," and I waved her in.

~~~***~~~

Hitch Hiker Alice

It had been a long trip and I needed a break from the Interstate. I was tired of truck stop food and the constant monotony of "straight ahead" driving. I saw the sign that said, "Wigginsville Next Exit" and on a whim I pulled off on the exit and saw the sign with the left pointing arrow and the words "Wigginsville 6 miles." I turned left to follow the arrow and six miles later I passed the city limit sign and began looking for a restaurant.

As I slowly cruised down Main Street looking at the businesses on either side of the street I spotted a sign that said, "Estelle's Café" and I pulled into the next open parking place. Estelle's was just what I was looking for. Home cooked meals, home baked pies and cakes and some pretty damned good coffee. When I left an hour later I was stuffed. I stopped at the Diamond Shamrock at the far edge of town, filled my tank and then drove back through town headed for the exit that would put me back on the four lane.

I got caught at the light in the middle of town and as I sat there, fingers drumming on the steering wheel while waiting for the light to change, a woman came running down the street on my right. I stopped watching the light and put my attention on her. She obviously wasn't wearing a bra under her top and the way her chest moved as she ran was a sight to behold. I was caught by surprise when she ran up to my car, pulled open the passenger side door and jumped in. As the door was closing I saw a man come running out a door, look both ways and see the woman getting in my car. He turned and ran toward us. The light changed and the car behind me beeped and I moved forward and started to ease my way over to the curb on the other side of the intersection. As soon as the woman was in my car she started talking.

"Please help me, please get me out of here" and as I pulled toward the curb she cried, "What are you doing? Don't stop, please get me away from here."

"Whoa up honey. I got no way of knowing whether that guy chasing you is a cop trying to arrest you or not. I'm not rushing into anything here."

"He's not a cop. You don't hear him hollering 'stop, police' do you?"

I looked back at the guy running toward us. If he was a cop he was unlike any other cop I had ever seen. He had so many piercings on his face that a magnet would have lifted him right off his feet. As he ran his coat flapped open and I saw the gun in the shoulder holster and I was already screeching away from the curb as she cried, "Please get me away from here."

As we passed the city limit sign I asked, "Are you going to tell me what this is all about?"

"You're better off not knowing."

"I don't think so honey. At this point the more I know the happier I'll be."

"Can't you just get me to a truck stop?"

"Doesn't work that way honey. Not trying to be melodramatic, but the guy chasing you got close enough to get a good look at me and at the car and most likely he was close enough to get my plate numbers. If somebody really serious is trying to get their mitts on you they as good as have me. What am I mixed up in and what do I need to be on the lookout for?"

"Let's just leave it at I'm running away."

"Suit yourself" I said as I took my foot off the gas and steered for the shoulder.

"What are you doing?"

"I'm pulling over to let you out and then I'm turning around and driving back into town to find out what I'm messed up in."

"No, no, please don't. I'll make it worth your while to keep on going."

"Oh yeah? How's that?"

"I've been told I'm pretty good and a lot of men have spent a lot of time trying to get their hands on these" and she lifted her top and showed me two of the firmest tits I'd ever seen, not big, but very firm. Get me a hundred miles from here and I'll fuck your brains out."

"Only if you tell me what this is all about."

"You can't just take the goods and let it go?"

"Sorry, but I can't. It's like I told you honey; they got my plate numbers and a description of my car so they as good as have me. The guy chasing you had a gun so if guys like that come looking for me I want to know what to expect."

"Shit! I lose either way I go."

"What do you mean?"

"I don't tell you and you put me out here and they probably are not far behind and they get me. I tell you and you'll turn around and take me back to keep from getting any more involved."

"Or I might just floor it and get us the hell down the road."

"I guess I don't have much of a choice."

"The guy chasing me is my husband's brother, but he's not the only one. If he found me it won't be long before there are others looking for me around here too."

"Can I get some clarity on that?"

"The FBI, the DEA, and the LAPD will be trying to get me too."

"Jesus lady, what did you do?"

"Nothing. Outside of marrying a crook, nothing."

"Then why in the hell is everyone after you?"

"Because they all think that I know something. The problem is that I don't. When I married Sam I thought he was a successful used car dealer, but it turns out that he and his brother Elmer had ties to organized crime in LA. Sam got busted holding dope and the mob, the Mafia, or whatever the hell they call themselves, sent a guy to tell me to keep quiet and they would take care of me if Sam got sent away.

"The guy they sent was an idiot and he misunderstood what he was supposed to do. He pulled a gun on me and was getting ready to use it, but he didn't see my sister when he walked in the house and she whacked him with a table lamp. We wrapped him up in duct tape and pushed him down the basement stairs. And I said, "fuck this shit" and went and packed a bag. While I was in the bedroom packing the bag the DEA showed up. My sister answered the door and they asked her if she was me and she said yes to buy me enough time to bail out the window. I heard them say "You'll have to come with us for questioning" just before I went out the window.

"I called Elmer to find out what the hell was going on and I told him what had happened and how the DEA had taken Denise. He told me what the guy was actually supposed to be there for and then he told me I should check into a hotel under an assumed name and call him the next day. The next day I called him and he told me that the FBI was looking for me too and that the LAPD wanted to ask me about the duct taped guy at the bottom of my basement steps with the broken neck.

"I changed motels every day and checked in with Elmer to find out what I should do next. One day he sounded different and asked me to meet him. I had a bad feeling so I went to the meet two hours early. An hour before the meet Elmer showed up with three other guys and all three went and hid. I knew then that they were going to do what the first guy didn't and I ran.

"That was four years ago and I've been living a nice quiet life in Wigginsville ever since. Until today that is. Luckily I saw Elmer before he saw me and I was able to grab my purse and my coffee can and run."

"Coffee can?"

"Yeah. No bank accounts, nothing with my Social Security number. Supposed to make it harder to find you. All my money was either in my purse or my coffee can in the cupboard."

We rode silently for the next five or six miles and then I asked, "How much money do you have?"

"Why?"

"Because I don't carry much cash with me when I travel on business. I mostly use credit cards, but credit card transactions can be traced."

"How much do I need?"

"Enough for a bus ticket."

"I can't do that. They would find out and be waiting at the bus stop when I got there."

"Yeah, but you won't be on the bus."

I knew that Trailways used Union 76 truck stops as terminals on the Interstate so we drove the hundred miles to get to the next one. I had Alice (we finally got around to introductions) use what cash she had to buy a ticket to the farthest point east that she had the money for and then we waited for the bus. Alice got on, making sure that the driver got a damned good look at those memorable tits of hers and then while he loaded luggage I distracted him and Alice snuck off the bus.

"Now we go across the street and get a motel room to hide you in while I call the cops."

"No cops. I can't go to the cops."

"No, but I have to. That's why I have to get you a room to hide in."

I paid cash for a one-night stay, gave a fake name and fake plate numbers on the registration card and then I went back to the truck stop and called the state police. It took them an hour to show up which worked out well considering the story I told. I told them exactly what happened and that I'd told her that we had to call the police.

"Hell honey, you can't have men with guns chasing after you."

I told them that we had argued about it and that I had pulled into the truck stop to use the bathroom.

"When I came out she was gone. I asked around to see if anyone had seen her and one guy told me that he had seen her climb up into a blue Peterbuilt just before it pulled out."

I gave them descriptions of Alice and the guy who was chasing her and after they left I left my car parked at the truck stop and walked back over to the hotel. I don't know if I'd done any good, but I hoped that I had accomplished three things; the hood was chasing the bus going east, the police were looking God knows where for a blue Peterbuilt and I was covered as far as the FBI and the DEA were concerned. If they ever called on me I could tell them where they could find a police report on the whole thing.

Alice was in the shower when I got to the motel room. I sat down on the bed and turned on the TV and started watching CNN. I didn't notice when the shower stopped running and I didn't even know she was through until I heard her say:

"You still have your clothes on."

"No reason to take them off."

"Oh yes there is. I have a debt to pay and clothes will only get in the way."

"I have no intention of holding you to that. I don't expect pay for helping someone in trouble."

"Doesn't matter what you want. I pay my debts and there is another reason besides."

I looked away from the TV and over at her.

"I haven't been laid since the day I ran from my house in LA and all I've been thinking about since I told you what I would do for your help has been grinding away in my mind. I'm so horny right now that if you don't work with me on this I'll rape you."

It proved to be a very long and exhausting night as Alice tried to make up for four years of going without sex. I am only a mortal man and at no time in my previous thirty-four years did I ever go more than three times in one night and only then through superhuman effort. Alice pulled energy reserves out of me that I never knew I had. We fucked and then she sucked me hard again. We fucked and then she sat on my face and played with my cock until I got hard again. We fucked and went sixty-nine until she got me hard again. And then we fucked some more. After the fifth time I just laid there and looked up at her and croaked, "No way, you've ruined me for life" and then she laughed at me and proved me wrong.

When I heard the maid's cart rattling down the hall I knew it was time to go. I went out first and looked around and I didn't see anyone who looked like they were watching so I went over to the truck stop, got my car, drove to a McDonald's and got half a dozen breakfast sandwiches and went back and picked up Alice. We got on the Interstate and as we drove we ate the sandwiches and it was a good thing because I soon found that I was going to need the energy.

Half an hour down the road Alice slid over next to me an unzipped my pants.

"You looking to get us killed?"

"Don't be silly lover. All you have to do is drive. I'm going to be doing all the work here."

I tried to concentrate on keeping the car going straight ahead, but her hot mouth was driving me crazy and I had to pull over and let her finish me off. Once back on the road she asked me to look for a place where I could pull off the road for some privacy.

"I shouldn't have done what I did. It just made me horny. I need to be fucked."

"Sweetie, if we keep this up we will never get out of this state. We need to put distance between this place and us. Buses and Peterbuilts won't keep them busy forever."

"Just a quickie lover. Something to take the edge off."

Sixty miles later we came to a rest area and I pulled in and parked well away from any other vehicles. I have never been overly fond of back seat sex because of the cramped feeling I get, but somehow it was different with Alice. With Alice there seemed to be a heat that just sucked you in and made you oblivious to whatever else was around.

It was not a quickie to take the edge off. It seemed to feed on itself; every stroke seemed to demand that two more follow it and when at last I came the heat of Alice's pussy would not let me leave. I soaked in her until the faint stirrings of life were again felt in my cock and then we did it again."

When we finally got back on the road Alice was quiet. I didn't say anything either as I concentrated on driving and on the thoughts running riot in my head. I wanted this woman. I wanted to keep her at my side forever, but I saw no way that I could ever make it happen. Once the sequence of events that put us together started, any relationship was doomed because of the possibility that Elmer had gotten my plate numbers.

That number gave them me and while I was sure that the bus trick and the police report would support me when whoever I ended up talking to came around I obviously couldn't have Alice there when they came and two things were certain – come they would, and I would never know when or how often.

Another hundred miles went by before I had an idea. I rolled it around in my head for another fifty and then I turned to Alice and said, "How fond are you of your face and hair?"

* * *

It was hideously expensive and it was time consuming, but it worked, or at least it has so far. Alice sat across the room and listened as I told my story to the twentieth FBI agent to come see me. The visits have gotten fewer and farther apart over the last three years and I'm looking forward to the day when they stop all together. For the last two years Alice, now known as Roberta, has been hiding in plain sight. Gone were the long blond hair and the cute button nose that had sat in the middle of a sensuous face and the trim figure. Now the hair is a dark brown and cut in a waifish style and an angular nose that looks like it has been broken sits in the middle of a face that is more striking than beautiful. The figure while still fairly trim is an eye catcher with the 38DD breasts on prominent display.

Gone also are the sedate conservative clothes. They have been replaced by tight skirts, low cut blouses and an assortment of Come Fuck Me pumps. Everything about her screams out "look at me" which is just the opposite of what someone who wants to hide would do. Plastic surgery, hair dye and silicone implants have made Alice invisible.

It took time, effort and a lot of money to make it happen. I put Alice in a motel when I got home. It was two weeks before I saw her again. Two weeks during which I went about my normal routine. I did notice a few new faces in the neighborhood and I did see what appeared to be the same car behind me several times, but I just ignored them. I went to work, saw customers, and went out on an occasional date.

One day during the second week two men came into my office and flashed badges. They were from the FBI and would I please accompany them downtown for some questions. I told my story, three times, and was shown several photos. I pointed to one and said that it was Alice and then I pointed to one of Elmer and said that he was the man I had seen chasing her. By the end of the second week I didn't see any more strange faces in the neighborhood or recognize cars following me.

The Monday of the third week I started out on my monthly road trip and went through all kinds of weird maneuvers to satisfy myself that I wasn't being followed and then I drove to the motel where I had put up Alice. The plan was that we would leave immediately and she would go on my road trip with me, but I hadn't considered the fact that Alice might have other plans. She started me off with a blow job and then it was fuck and suck off and on for the next twenty-four hours. It was a memorable time for me in that it was the first time I'd ever had anal sex. It turned out that Alice loved anal sex and I asked her it that was true why she didn't have me do it during our first time.

"You were new to me lover. Not everyone likes doing it and there are some who think it is pretty degenerate and perverted. I was in no position to do anything that might have made you run away and leave me."

It was ten the next morning when I staggered out to the car.

For the next six months that was what we did. She would go on my road trips with me, spend the nights trying to fuck me to death, and I would put her in a motel when we got back. Arrangements were made, the surgery was done and one day Roberta came home with me.

One week later we had our first test. Two men, an FBI agent and an agent of the DEA came by with a few questions. I invited them in and when they saw Roberta they asked if we could talk in private.

"That won't be necessary. Roberta and I are getting married and I'm not going to have any secrets from her."

They glanced at her, shrugged their shoulders and asked their questions.

Alice and I won't be getting married of course. She is still married to Sam and can't get a divorce because of the paper trail it would leave. Our three years together has been great as far as I was concerned and when the trouble came it didn't come from any of the government alphabet agencies or the mob. It came from an unexpected direction and I found myself tested as never before.

I had spent a long time looking over my shoulder since meeting Alice, but when the trouble came it was not in the form of an FBI agent with a warrant or even a goombah with a gun. No, it was in the form of a dumpy looking businessman with a briefcase.

A customer of mine had flown into town and had called me and asked me to meet him for lunch at the motel where he was staying. By coincidence it was the motel where I had been putting Alice when we returned from my road trips.

I was sitting in the coffee shop with my customer when I happened to see Alice walk in the front door. She walked directly to the door that said "Manager" on it and without knocking she opened the door and went in. Darrel and I had finished eating and there was no reason for us to stay any longer, but something told me that I needed to stay there and keep an eye on that door.

"You know Darrel, I think I've changed my mind and I will have some dessert. I think I'll try some of that New York Cheese Cake after all."

I was half way through the wedge of cheesecake when the door opened and Alice came out followed by a short, fat guy carrying a briefcase. Alice said something to him and he gave her a nervous smile and then the two of them headed down the corridor that led to the first floor rooms.

Alice was home and fixing dinner when I got there. She turned to greet me when I walked into the kitchen and gave me a big smile.

"You want dessert first?"

"I don't know, what's for dessert?"

"Silly man" she said as she grabbed my tie and led me to the bedroom.

Over a late dinner I asked her how her day had gone.

"Nothing exciting. Watched some soaps most of the day and worked a few cross-word puzzles."

Uh huh, and that was your twin sister I saw at the motel.

The next day I didn't go to work and I was sitting down the block from the house when Alice came out. I followed her back to the motel and

I was behind a magazine rack in the gift shop watching the manager's door when the man I recognized as the manager came out with Alice. He went to the front desk and got a key and brought it back and handed it to her. He said something, she nodded a yes and then she headed down the corridor in the direction of the rooms.

I was outside, parked where I could see her car, when she came out an hour and a half later and I followed her back home. I let her get inside before I pulled up and parked. I was a little on the quiet side as I let myself into the house and closed the door behind me. Alice was sitting on the toilet using her douche bag when I walked up to the bathroom door. Until that moment I wasn't at all sure of what had been going on. The little dumpy man could have been taking statements maybe. For all I knew Alice might have gotten tired of running and was now cooperating with the law in some way. But you don't need to douche after just talking to someone.

I just stood there looking at Alice for a minute and then I turned and walked away. I was in the kitchen getting a beer out of the fridge when Alice came into the room.

"It isn't what you think lover."

"It isn't? Well let's just look at it from my point of view shall we? I see you heading for a motel room with a short, dumpy looking guy yesterday – a day by the way that you said you stayed home and watched soaps – and today I followed you to the same motel and watched the manager give you a key following which you headed for a room. So, you going to tell me that it isn't what I think, that two and two don't equal four?"

She stood looking at me for several moments and then she turned to walk out of the room.

"Where are you going?"

"To pack."

"You would rather go pack than talk to me?"

"I've nothing to say that you want to hear and if I did talk you would probably throw me out anyway."

She headed for the bedroom and I finished my beer and got up and followed her.

She had a suitcase on the bed and was dragging stuff out of the closet. I stood and watched for a bit and then I said:

"I hate to make this sound like it's an "All about me" thing, but haven't I been through enough shit with and for you to at least get an explanation?"

"Straight up lover? I've been hooking."

"I don't understand."

"A hooker, a prostitute, a play for pay girl. I've been fucking for money."

"I know what a hooker is, what I don't understand is why."

The same thing that got me into trouble in the first place – wanting to stay away from cops."

I made a 'come on, gimme' motion with my hands.

"I'm walking around that fucking motel in my heels and revealing clothing and the manager comes up to me and says he's not going to have hookers dealing out of his place, at least not as long as he wasn't getting something out of it. I tried to convince him I wasn't a hooker but he wouldn't buy it. He told me to step into his office and we would discuss it. I told him we had nothing to discuss and he pointed to the front door where a cop car just happened to be sitting."

"In my office now" he said, "or I go tell them I've had complaints from some of the guests about you trying to hustle them."

"You were out of town and I didn't know how to reach you and I didn't want anything to do with the cops so I went into his office. He wanted a blow job to cement our new business relationship and I've been taking care of whoever he sets me up with ever since."

"And you just went along with it?"

"Yes, I just went along with it."

"Why? You could have told me and I would have gotten you out of there."

"Truth time?"

"Of course."

"There were a couple of reasons why lover. One, I needed something to do while you were gone. Two, I wanted the money and last, but not least, I wanted the sex. You know what the most amazing thing about me is lover? That I was able to hide out in Wigginsville for four years and do without any sex while I was there. I spent all my time worrying that if I got in a relationship it might somehow trip me up"

She walked over to the dresser, got her purse, took something out of it and tossed it to me. It was a passbook to a savings account and it was in my name.

"That's where I put the money I got for sex. I figure I owe you a ton. I owe you for my new face, I owe you for my new tits and most of all, I owe you for my life."

"I looked at the figure in the book, "Are you out of your mind? This is almost four times what I paid for your surgeries."

"The surgeries maybe, but don't try to put a cost on my life."

I just stood there staring at her. "Don't look at me like that lover, say something."

"I don't know what to say Alice."

"Roberta."

"What?"

"Roberta, you're supposed to be calling me Roberta, remember?"

"Oh, sorry. I suppose that I'm just stunned by the rather casual way you are treating this."

"No surprise there lover, at least not to me. That's what I was when I met Sam. A little higher priced than now, but that's what I was – a call girl. I did it then for the same reason I'm doing it now; I loved the sex and I got paid for it."

She paused for several seconds and then, "So, should I keep on packing?"

* * *

That was five years ago and a lot has happened since then. The bottom line was that her hooking hadn't hurt me any so I told Roberta if she wanted to hook go ahead and she did. A year after Roberta ran Sam was found guilty and sentenced to eight to ten years in prison. He was out in five and a half on good behavior. When Roberta read about it in the paper she made some phone calls and found out where he was and went to see him.

She didn't tell me before she did it. I came home and found a note telling me not to worry, that she would be in touch. She was gone for nine days. She called me every night just long enough to tell me she was all right, but couldn't talk.

The tenth day I came home to find her in the kitchen fixing dinner. All she had on were a pair of high heels and an apron. She smiled at me and said, "Dessert first lover" and she grabbed me by the tie and pulled me along behind her into the bedroom. Every time I tried to talk she said, "Hush lover. Make love now, we can talk later." Over a very, very late dinner I got the whole story.

She had found out where Sam was and then had called him and asked him if it was safe to come see him. He had blown up on her wanting to know where she had been, why she hadn't gone his bail, why she had never visited him in prison or jail and on and on. She told him what had happened and suddenly he got real silent.

"They did that to you? Elmer didn't tell me any of that."

"Elmer is the one they sent to do it Sam" and then she told him about the meeting that Elmer had set up and what she'd seen and why she'd run.

They made arrangements to meet and she warned him that she didn't look the same anymore. They met and then spent the next five days trying to fuck each other to death.

"Hey lover, don't look at me like that" she said when she saw my face after telling me about the five days. "Not once during this entire affair did I say that I didn't love Sam. I did and I still do."

At the end of five days Sam had made some phone calls and he and Alice had gone to some meetings with various people, apologies were made, restitution was offered and several people were severely chastised for over reacting. The most severely chastised was Elmer. Sam broke every bone in his body and suggested that when he got out of the hospital he disappear and never allow himself to be seen by Sam again.

"No, no I haven't."

"Think about it. What were you doing and what are you doing now?"

"I don't know what you mean."

"Okay, since I don't know what your circumstances were and I have to assume that the Army has changed some since my day I'll give it to you from my side.

"When I was drafted in 1942 there was none of this two year bullshit. When they took you it was 'For the war plus six months.' Then they take you to a training camp and they train you sixteen hours a day to kill people and destroy things. You learn to use rifles, pistols, BARs, machine guns, mortars, hand grenades, bayonets and knives. Then you finish basics and are assigned to a unit and the training goes on. It never lets up; this is how you kill, this is how you blow this up, this is how you tear this down. This is your enemy. Learn to hate him because he is evil personified and then kill him every chance you get.

"Then you find yourself in a landing craft approaching a beach. Bullets are clanging off the hull, artillery bursts are going off all around you. The ramp goes down and you find yourself in a living hell as men are dying all around you. You fight your way off the beach and for the next six months it is hedge row to hedge row, town after town, storming pillboxes, kicking down doors and tossing in grenades, fighting house to house and all the time men are falling all around you wounded and dying.

"They finally pull you off the line and send you back to a rest area and just about the time you stop wetting your pants every time you hear a loud noise they load you on trucks and send you back up to the line and it starts all over again. Suddenly one day it stops. It is like someone threw a switch. One minute you are being shot at and two seconds later it is peace and quiet. You get loaded on a troop ship and twenty-one days later you are back in the USA and two weeks later you are standing at a train

I'd taken my discharge at Fort Lewis in November of 1953 after coming home from spending a sixteen-month tour of duty in Korea. I'd come home to a family that had missed me and who had welcomed me home with home coming parties and family get-togethers. My sister's current boyfriend gave me a lead on a job where he worked and I applied, got the job and started to get on with my life.

But something was missing. I couldn't quite get into civilian life. Stopping with the guys after work for a beer was boring and tame. Even the few dates I went on seemed uninteresting.

I didn't know what the matter was with me, but someone else did – my father.

He and I really didn't get along and as far as I was concerned it was all his fault. He had come home from War Two, stayed with my mom and me for about two months and then he split. One day he left for work and never came home. Six months later he was back. He and my mom disappeared into their bedroom and I heard them talking most of the night and in the morning it seemed as if she had forgiven him, but I never did.

I was still living at home and one night I got home from work and found him sitting at the kitchen table waiting for me with a couple of beers. He opened one and pushed it toward me and motioned for me to sit down. We looked at each other in silence for several minutes and then he said:

"Figured it out yet?"

"Figured out what?"

"Just what it is that seems out of kilter with your life? Why everything seems just a little bit off and you can't quite put your finger on it?"

That was exactly what I was feeling; how could he know?

Hitch Hiker Amy

"My trousers fell to the floor and her eyes widened as she saw my proud tower of flesh. She stared in fascination as I climbed on the bed and positioned my thick, eight-inch piece of man meat at the entrance to her tunnel of love. Suddenly, as if coming out of a trance, she cried out, 'No, we can't, we must not. It would kill my husband if he found out.'

"Hush girl, you know that you want this."

"Oh god I do, I really do, but this is just so wrong."

"This will make it right. I said as I pushed my hard pole into her quivering quim."

"Can you believe it? Proud tower of flesh? Tunnel of love? I'm telling you that real people do not talk like that. Real people don't write shit like that. The letters in these magazines are all bullshit man. They are made up by people who work at the magazine."

Andy waved the copy of Penthouse Letters that he had been reading and said, "These stories are phony as shit too." He leafed through the magazine and stopped at a page, "Here's one. A housewife whose husband is out of town on business takes her laundry to the Laundromat. According to the story she has never been unfaithful. While she's doing the wash a guy comes in to wash his stuff. He asks her if he should use bleach on something and she tells him no and then a paragraph later she is on her knees sucking his cock and then she goes back to his room with him and they fuck for the three days her husband is gone."

"I'm telling you guys, all this is phony shit. Things like that just don't happen in real life" and as all the other guys sitting there agreed with him I just sat there and thought, "You are wrong Andy, oh so wrong. Things like that do happen in the real world" and I let my memory take me back to the spring of 1954.

The meetings over there were another three days of non-stop sex, "And now here I am."

I just stared at her while I tried to get my mind around what she'd just told me.

She looked at me, "Well, say something."

"You disappear on me for ten days and have eight days of non-stop sex? What the hell do you expect me to say?"

"Glad to have you home would be nice."

"You lost me. You still love Sam, you've just had eight days of sex with him and you are here. What did I miss?"

"I admit that it might be a little unorthodox, but I happen to be deeply in love with two men and I do not intend to give either of them up. So, here's the plan. When you are on the road I am Sam's. When you get home I am yours. You get the better of the deal because, at least if the last five years are any indication, you will have me thirty-one weeks and Sam will only have me for twenty-one. Although I did tell Sam I would talk to you to see if I could talk you into an even split. He won't push because he's grateful that you saved my ass and he loves the new tits you bought me. Look on the bright side lover, I won't be hooking any more when you are on the road because I'll have Sam to keep me company."

I just sat there in stunned amazement and stared at her. She stood up and reached across the table and took my hand. "Come on lover" she said as she pulled me to my feet, "Let's go to bed and I'll work my magic. You will love this new deal to death when I get done with you."

~~~***~~~

station with a government travel voucher in one hand and your discharge papers in the other

"Three days later you are home, but home to what? A nine to five job, nights sitting on the couch listening to Amos and Andy or George Burns and Gracie Allen? The days are dull and boring after what you have just been through. Some men just can't go from months and months of stark terror to orderly calm overnight.

"That's where the Army, Navy and Marines fail us. They wind us up, but whenever what they wound us up for is over, they cut us loose. There is no period of winding down, of getting what they pumped into you out of your system. One day you are clearing a house room to room with grenades and bayonets and then suddenly you are in a house and fixing the storm windows. Some made the adjustment, but a lot of us didn't."

"That's why you left us?"

"I had to get away. I had to, for lack of a better way of saying it, cleanse my system. I had to get rid of the insane urge to settle every argument with a vertical butt stroke. I was seething with violence and I had to get it out of me."

"So what did you do when you were gone?"

"I'm not going into that. A lot of what I did I'm not proud of, but to boil it down I looked for dangerous jobs, jobs that would let me work the bad shit out of my system. It took a while, but one day I woke up and said, "I could get killed doing this shit" and I knew then it was time to try and come home. Luckily for me your mother is one hell of an understanding woman.

"I see a lot of what I felt when I came home in you. The shooting in your war ended in July of '53 so you had a couple of months to adjust, but you still seem to have – I don't know – a need to let off steam."

"So what do you suggest I do?"

"Hell, I don't know. Take up sky diving, go over Niagara Falls in a barrel, just do something that will burn whatever is still inside of you out of you."

Not too long after that I saw Marlon Brando in "The Wild Ones" and I don't to this day know exactly why, but at the point in the picture where the town girl says to Brando, "What are you rebelling against Johnny?" and Brando replied, "I don't know, whaddya got?" I knew that I needed to get a motorcycle and go screaming down the highway with my hair on fire. It would be exciting and exhilarating and just maybe dangerous enough to burn out what my father thought he saw in me.

I bought a used 1947 Harley and set out to run up and down the roads as fast as I could. It was not an uneventful time in my life. I pushed that bike to the limit and several times I had the cops chasing me for being so far over the speed limit that my speedometer was pegged out. But I was on my Harley and I was invincible and I ran from them and I never did get caught.

One day I was in a gas station filling up when another rider came in. He said he had seen me riding around the neighborhood and he introduced himself and we started riding together. He belonged to a club and he talked me into joining and soon I was riding all over the state with a group of guys. One night we were sitting in a tavern drinking beer and trying to decide where we were going to go next when a guy and a girl walked in and sat down in a booth. It was dark in the place so I did not get a good look at them, but it was obvious from the loud talking coming from their booth that they were not happy with each other.

Me and the guys got up and left. My 74 didn't want to start right off and the other guys had already pulled out of the lot when I heard, "Most of the others had girls riding with them. Don't you have a girl to ride with?"

I turned and looked and saw that it was the girl who had been arguing with the guy in the tavern. Not bad looking, but no raving beauty either. She did have a stupendous set of tits though. I found out later that they were 38DDs.

"No" I said, "I don't have a girl to ride with me."

"Sure you do. Scoot up and make room for me."

I kicked the bike one more time and it roared to life, she got on behind me and I tore out of the lot and cranked it on to try and catch up with my buddies. Three miles down the road a car came up behind me flashing its headlights and blowing its horn. I turned to look at it (mirrors were 'sissy' things back then) and the girl said:

"It's my husband, lose him."

My first instinct was to dump her off the bike – I didn't need to be getting into it with no husband – but at the speed we were going it wouldn't have been a good thing. And then I thought about how good it felt to have those 38's boring holes in my back as she held on tight so I twisted the throttle and left the car eating my dust. Three minutes later I caught up with the pack and roared past them and they picked up speed and came up on my tail. There was a crossroad coming up and I asked her if she wanted me to let her off to wait for him.

"Hell no. Turn left, he'll go right thinking that I'm heading home."

I hung a left and twenty miles later we came to a tavern on a lake and I pulled into the parking lot. The others pulled in behind me and as they were putting down their kickstands I saw their curious glances. I also saw the apprehension in the girl's eyes as she looked around at them and I knew right away what she was thinking.

"Relax" I said. "They will if you want them to, but you will have to make it very clear to them that is what you want. Is that what this is all about?"

"No, no it isn't. I'm pissed at my husband, but not that pissed."

"Care to bring me up to speed?"

"I just found out that Mike has been fucking my cousin Sally and I decided that if he can screw around so can I. I told him that and he laughed at me and told me that I wasn't the type to do something like that. When your gang got up to leave I saw that you didn't have a girl so here I am."

"So it wasn't my rugged manliness that attracted you? I'm just a piece of meat that you can use to get back at your husband?"

"Whatever. You going to turn me down?" She lifted her sweater up over her head and took off her bra, "You going to walk away from these?"

The rest of the guys were hooting and whistling as I stared at her tits. They were perfect. No sag to them at all and they stuck straight out like the tips of two torpedoes. I looked from them to her face and then back down at those marvelous tits and said:

"No, no I'm not, not in this lifetime anyway."

I brought the others up to date on what was happening and then we went into the tavern and shot pool and drank beer for a couple of hours and then we headed for home.

I had my own apartment by then and I led Amy through it to the bedroom. I turned on the light and turned to her:

"You don't have to do this. You can just tell him that you did."

"Oh no, I have to do it. I have to get even with that bastard. Also, I have to prove him wrong. He said that I couldn't do it so I have to prove to myself that I can" and with that she started to take off her clothes. She cupped her tits in her hands and squeezed them as she offered them to me.

"You like? My nipples are very sensitive and I can actually orgasm when they are licked and sucked. Care to try?"

I made love to those tits. I licked, sucked and slobbered all over them and she squealed with delight. The harder I worked on them the louder she squealed and moaned and then she did have an orgasm and don't think that didn't make me feel like a stud horse.

"My turn now baby. My husband says I'm quite good at this" and she sank to her knees in front of me and gave me the hottest blow job I'd ever received. Why her stupid fuck of a husband wasted his time on someone else when he had her I'll never know. I was so worked up from working on her tits that she got me off in no time. After she had swallowed every drop I had and had licked me clean she said:

"Not to worry baby, we aren't even close to being done.

She pulled me up onto the bed and pushed me down on my back and then she straddled me. She lifted my limp cock up and then she surrounded it with those stupendous melons and tit fucked me until I was hard again.

It was thirty-six hours before we came out of the bedroom to do anything other than eat or go to the toilet and it might have gone on longer had I been able to get it up any more. She was totally insatiable. We fucked and then she would suck my dick to get me hard again. This happened four times before we fell asleep curled up around each other. Three hours later she woke me up with another blow job and when she saw that I was awake she slid forward and sat on my face and I did what was expected of me until she pulled herself away from me.

"I guess my husband doesn't know me as well as he thought he did. I am not only capable of doing this I have discovered that I like doing this. I want to do something that I've never let my husband do to me. Would you fuck me in my ass?"

When we finally got to the point where my cock just would not respond we fell asleep and slept for ten hours. When I woke up she was on the phone.

"That is up to you," she was saying. "You just have to know that I won't put up with it. You got away with it this time because I decided to pay you back in kind. If it happens again I'll just leave and that will be the end of it. So, with that in mind should I come home or do you just want to go ahead and call it quits now?"

"I don't know, it is up to him. If he is finished with me I'll be home sometime today, but if he still wants more of my pussy it may be a day or two."

"You should have thought of that before you decided to fuck Sally."

"I'll ask him."

She turned to me, "How much longer would you like me to stay?"

"The rest of my life sounds like a start."

"It may be a couple of days yet Mike. I'll give you a call."

She turned to me again, "You want breakfast first to build up your strength, or do you want to work up an appetite first?"

At the end of the fifth day she called her husband and told him that they were even. "We can try to put things back together now if you want to, just remember – do it again and I won't waste time getting even, I'll just be gone."

When I pulled up in front of her place he was sitting on the front porch waiting. She kissed me and climbed off the bike and headed for the house and he got up and ran to her, hugged her and then picked her up and carried her into the house. I motored off wishing that he would have had all of her stuff stacked outside on the porch so I could have taken her back home with me. She had my phone number and I told her to call me if things didn't work out and that I'd come back and get her, but I never heard from her again.

The motorcycle and the things I did while I owned it took whatever it was inside me that I had brought home from Korea and killed it off. My father's confession and my understanding of it healed the rift between us and two years later I met and married the woman who celebrated our thirty-fifth anniversary with me last month.

Andy tossed the magazine onto the center of the break room table and the thump it made when it hit brought me out of my reverie. "It's rubbish, all rubbish" he said again and all I could do was smile.

~~~***~~~

Hitch Hiker Shauna

It might have been going on for a while, but I first noticed it at mile marker 197 just west of Brady on Interstate 80. A red late model Dodge Intrepid seemed to be playing some kind of game with me. It would be behind me for a while and then it would pull out to pass and blow by me at 85 or 90 miles an hour and a quarter mile down the road it would pull back into my lane and slow down.

The speed limit was 70 and I had my cruise control set on 76 and I was trusting that no cop was going to bother me for going 6 miles over. At 76 I would slowly creep up on the Dodge and eventually I would have to hit my brake, which would take me out of cruise control, or I would have to swing out and pass. Unless there was traffic I always opted for the swing out and pass option and then a quarter mile or so down the road I would pull back into the right lane and the cycle would repeat itself.

About the fifth time it happened I glanced over at the driver of the Dodge as it flew by and saw that the driver was an extremely attractive young woman. After that fifth time I began to think that what she was doing was deliberate and I started trying to figure out just what it was that she was doing. Try as I might I could not come up with an explanation.

It went on for another forty miles or so and then finally she pulled out, passed me doing 90 and pulled back in front of me only to get off the Interstate at the 133 exit. Weird, I thought, but it had been a distraction from the long and boring ride across I-80.

* * *

It was maybe twenty minutes later and darkness had fallen when I noticed a set of headlights coming up from behind at a high rate of speed. There were no flashing lights so I didn't think that it was a cop after somebody and then, suddenly, the red Dodge roared by me and a quarter mile later pulled in front of me and the game began again.

I was in the lead when I swung off of I-80 onto I-76 and I was surprised when I saw the Dodge follow along. I was even more surprised when the Dodge followed me off I-76 at Julesburg and into the Flying J truck stop where I had planned to get a bite to eat and fuel up for the final leg into Denver.

I saw the Dodge park at the far end and no one got out while I gassed up. I pulled away from the pump and pulled up in front of the restaurant and went inside and took a seat. I was looking at the menu when someone slid onto a chair across from me and I looked up and into the biggest brown eyes I had ever seen. They were set in a face that was more striking than beautiful, but the face topped a body to die for.

"Hi. I'm Shauna. Mind if I join you?"

Like I would say no, right? I introduced myself and then I asked her what she had playing at with me for the last two hundred miles.

"Just trying to break the monotony of the long haul across 80. I half expected you to follow me when I got off for gas."

"What would have happened if I had?"

"I don't know, but it might have been fun."

"What kind of fun?"

"We'll never know will we?"

"Where are you headed?"

"I'm supposed to be on my way to Sacramento, California."

"You should have stayed on 80; it would have taken you right into Sacramento."

"I know. I'm just not all that sure that I want to go to Sacramento anymore."

Just then a man approached us and said, "Just what do you think you are doing asshole?"

I looked up, "Are you talking to me?"

"Yeah you dick breath, just what the fu…"

He never finished what he was going to say because I tossed my glass of water into his face and when his hands instinctively went up to cover his eyes I grabbed the front of his shirt and pulled his face down into the table. He fell in a heap on the floor. The manager came running up:

"I don't want no trouble in here. Take your beef outside"

"Just leaving" I said and I got up and headed for the door. Shauna was right behind me and when we got outside she said, "Sorry about that."

"Sorry about what?"

"What just happened? I thought he was asleep in the back seat."

"You know him?"

"He was the reason that I was going to Sacramento and he is also the reason I wasn't sure that I wanted to go to Sacramento."

"I think you lost me there."

"He was my fiancée and we were on the way to Sacramento so I could meet his folks and make wedding plans."

"Was your fiancée?"

"You learn a lot about someone when you are cooped up in a car with them for eighteen hundred miles. By the time we hit Kearny I wasn't sure that I really wanted to go through with the wedding."

"And now?"

"You got room in your car for me and three suitcases?"

I helped Shauna move her stuff from the Intrepid into my car and through the window of the restaurant I saw people helping Shauna's boyfriend up off the floor.

"You going to say goodbye to him?

"Nah! He'll figure it out eventually," she said as she tossed the car keys onto the front seat of the Dodge.

"Let's get out of here."

* * *

We pulled out of the Flying J and got on 76. The first ten miles were traveled in silence as Shauna looked out the passenger side window at the dark countryside. Finally I broke the silence.

"Having second thoughts? We are still close enough to turn around and go back. He will probably still be there."

"No, no second thoughts. Troy has always been a jealous and possessive asshole and I think that is what attracted me to him in the first place. To go from a life where no one gave a shit about me to where I had a man who thought so much of me that he wanted to own me and keep others away from me was somehow comforting. Remember when I said you learn a lot about someone when you are cooped up with them for eighteen hundred miles?"

I nodded a yes.

"I wasn't talking about Troy, I was talking about me. By the Illinois/Indiana state line I knew I was making a mistake. I'm just not the marrying kind. I'm not a girl who can tie herself down to just one man. You know what I mean?"

"No, I'm afraid that I don't."

Shauna slid across the seat until she was next to me and said, "I like cock too much sweetie" as her hand went to my zipper. "I'm too much of a slut to stay true to one man and I knew it, but for a while I convinced myself that I could change and that Troy and I could build a life together. By Omaha I knew I was kidding myself. When I made that last gas stop on 80 I was hoping that you would follow me. I was going to fuck you on your back seat while Troy slept in the car next to us."

By then she had my erection out and was stroking me and I was debating whether to continue driving or to pull over to the side of the road. Common sense won out and I pulled over onto the shoulder of the road just as her hot mouth closed around my cock. It did not take me long to realize that Troy's loss was my gain.

Her mouth was as soft as warm butter and her tongue and lips felt like feathers as they danced around the head of my dick. She licked the underside and kissed the length until she was back to the head and then she looked up at me, smiled and swallowed it. Her head bobbed up and down three times and then she had her nose in my pubic hairs as I was deep-throated for the first time in my life. She worked me until she had me ready to cum and then she backed off for a minute or so and then she went after me again. She did that three times until I could no longer hold back and when I came it was so hard that I was surprised I didn't blow the back of her head off.

After she had licked me clean she looked up at me and smiled, "Will that hold you until we get to your place? You are going to let me stay with you for a while aren't you?"

I did let her stay with me and for five weeks I enjoyed the wildest sex imaginable. Shauna was insatiable. Every morning she woke me with a blow job and sent me out the door well fucked to greet the new day. She would wait naked for me when I got home from work at night and on some nights we never even got to have dinner. Once she even took a cab down to where I worked so she could have lunch with me and when I asked her where she would like to have lunch she said, "The back seat of your car. What I'm really hungry for right now is a nice hard tube steak if you take my meaning." I did, but not being an exhibitionist I took her to a hotel instead of my back seat.

Shauna's big thing was having her pussy eaten just after I fucked her; she said that having cum eaten out of her was such a turn on that she always had an orgasm when it happened. Given that she was giving me so much I felt that it behooved me to give her back something so, much as I hated the taste, I did what she wanted. If we screwed in the morning and I didn't have time to do it before going to work she would try and hold as much in her during the day as she could so I could do it as soon as I got home that night.

More than any other girl I had ever known, Shauna was always hot, wet and ready. The day she came down to the office and we went to the hotel she lay back on the bed and pulled apart her pussy lips so that I could see that she had saved my morning leavings for me. She gave me a wicked little grin and said, "I plan on having tube steak, but I have cream pie for you. Come on baby, play vacuum cleaner for me."

I went to my knees and buried my face in the wet mess and licked until she cried out, "Fuck me now baby, fuck me now."

I never made it back to work that afternoon.

* * *

Life was good and, silly me, I began to think that Shauna and I might have a future together, but Shauna had told me what she was and I had forgotten. I came home from work early one day and found Shauna on my bed and sliding up and down on some stranger's erection. I watched for a minute or two as they fucked without noticing me and then I went out to the kitchen and fixed myself a stiff drink. As I sipped it I thought of all the times I had come home from work and she had been hot and wet and waiting for me to go down on her and I almost barfed.

Thirty minutes later a naked Shauna came out of the bedroom hustling her dressed lover along. "Hurry sweetie, we need to get you out of here before he gets home" she was saying and then she saw me.

"Oops. I guess there is no hurry now, but you still need to leave."

She walked the man to the door and when it closed behind him she turned to face me.

"I'm sorry baby, but I did tell you what I was. I guess I've overstayed my welcome huh?"

"Yes Shauna, I guess you have."

I watched her pack and then I drove her out to the airport and dropped her off. I have no idea where she flew off to and I never heard from her again.

~~~***~~~

Hitch Hiker Elise

It had been one of my longer hauls - Denver to Seattle to Los Angeles to St. Louis and then back to Denver. I had stopped at the Flying J Travel Plaza in Salina, Kansas for food and fuel and I was browsing the aisles in the convenience store when I noticed a stunning brunette standing at the bank of pay phones. What intrigued me was the way that she was dressed - mini-skirt and 'come fuck me' high heels. Not the normal attire you see in a truck stop unless the lady is a hooker. But this woman didn't really look like a hooker even though she was dressed like one.

Most of the hookers that I had seen at truck stops, while not bad looking, had a certain hard edge to them that the brunette didn't have. It might be that she was new at the game and hadn't hardened up yet, or it might be that I totally misread what I was seeing, but either way she was way too nice for me to pass up. If she was a foxy lady who had stopped for a bite to eat on the way home from a party I might get my face slapped, but hey - no pain, no gain, right?

I walked over to her and waited until she hung up the phone. She finished her call, turned to me and gave me what I can only call a "What do you want" look and I jumped in feet first.

"You looking for some company?"

The look on her face turned to one of puzzlement and then understanding and I was almost sure that I had misjudged and I clenched my teeth and waited for the blow. She took a quick look around and then said, "Just what did you have in mind?"

I relaxed my jaw, thought 'hot damn' and said, "I thought that maybe we could take a little walk out to my rig and check out the sleeper."

She took another look around and then said, "Let's go."

I could feel a hundred pair of eyes on us as we walked across the lot to my truck and I knew that most of them were eating their hearts out - she was that nice! Once in the sleeper she said, "By the way, my name is Elise. You didn't ask, so I assume you don't care, but I am a little expensive. I get a hundred dollars for a blow job and two hundred for a straight fuck. If you want my ass it's another hundred and fifty. If you want all three as a package deal it is three seventy-five."

That got my attention in a hurry. I was used to fifty dollar blow jobs and a half and half for one fifty, but I knew that I would never get a shot at something this nice again so I said, "Blow job and a straight fuck" and I pulled out my wallet. As I counted out the money into her hand I commented, "Just my luck. Fifty bucks short of being able to get all three."

She grinned at me, "If you want my ass sailor, I'll take your watch for the difference."

I didn't even hesitate - I peeled that twenty-dollar Casio off and handed it to her with the rest of my cash. I might not eat for two days, but it would be worth it. She stripped and I almost came just looking at her tits. I asked her to leave her high heels on and as soon as I was undressed she went for my cock. I was surprised when she twisted around so I could taste her pussy while she sucked my cock. Just before her mouth closed on me she said, "Do a good job sailor and I might give you back your watch."

I buried my face in her bush and did my absolute best to get that cheap Casio back while she gave me the best head I'd ever gotten. She had me ready to blow in minutes and knowing that whores don't swallow I warned her that I was ready to come. She took her mouth off me long enough to say, "Just keep eating me sugar" and she went back to sucking me and when I came she clamped her lips around me and gulped down everything I shot. She kept on working on me with her mouth until I was hard again and then she rolled off me and spread her legs, "Hurry up sailor, time is money."

I got on top of her and pushed myself in. She locked her legs behind mine and her hands grabbed my ass and pulled me to her, "Come on sailor, get your money's worth, fuck me hard."

For a whore she sure was tight and she was one hell of an actress. She made me believe that I was really turning her on and getting her off. She faked an orgasm that could have won her an Academy Award, but hell, I didn't care because I was looking down into one of the most beautiful faces that I had ever seen. I knew that the memory of this evening was going to be with me for the rest of my life. It took me almost ten minutes before I was ready to come and about a nano-second before I shot my load I realized that she hadn't asked me to put on a rubber. I began to think that my initial assessment of her was right - she was new at this and she hadn't yet learned that whores were not supposed to swallow and that they always used rubbers. Hell, I might even be her first customer! I stayed in her, slowly pumping, until I was soft.

She was looking up at me with a look I couldn't decipher and then she said, "You want to earn some of your money back?"

This was a new one on me so I said, "What's the catch?"

"No catch sailor, I just like to have my pussy eaten after I've been fucked and not many guys want to do it when I have cum in it. Clean me out and I'll give you back a hundred. Oh by the way, you've already earned your watch back."

I looked down at her in amazement. I pinched myself to see if I was dreaming and it hurt so I knew that I was awake. The only other possibility was that I had died and gone to Heaven. A whore with a gorgeous face and a killer body, who swallowed, didn't use rubbers and who was willing to pay me to eat her pussy? No way! Not in real life. But dream or Heaven I didn't care and I dove in. I love to eat pussy and it's something that my ex-wife used to tell me that I did well and I never have minded when they had cum in them. Well, that's a lie. I didn't mind when they had MY cum in them, but I wasn't all that keen on them when they had someone else's - that's why she was my ex-wife. Anyway, I worked on Elise's cum muffin for a good five minutes while she bucked her hips up at me and moaned.

By the end of that five minutes my cock was hard again and she giggled and said, "I guess you are ready for my ass now" and she got up on her knees and put her head on my pillow. I slid my thumb in her pussy to get a little juice on it and then I worked on her rosebud a bit to open it up and then I poked her pussy a couple of times to get my dick wet. Slowly I began to work my dick into her asshole and she groaned, "Easy sailor, easy. Let me get used to it."

I took my time; I was in no hurry because I wanted her around as long as I could manage. I was halfway in when a cell phone chirped. I knew it wasn't mine because mine beeped. Elise reached for her purse and pulled her phone out and I stopped plunging in and out of her while she took the call.

"Hello?"

"Out on the lot with a truck driver. He's showing me his sleeper. (She giggled)"

"What do you think I'm doing?"

"No baby, I'm doing what you always said you wanted."

"That's right. I'm finally doing it. Right now he's buried in my ass." (I felt her body stiffen)

"You miserable fucking rotten cocksucking bastard! You've begged me for this for five goddamned years and now you are calling me a whore? Well fuck you Stan!" She disconnected and threw the phone at her purse.

"Trouble" I asked.

"Just fuck me sailor, fuck me hard. We can talk later."

I went back to stroking into her butt and in a minute or so she was back to moaning, "Oh yes oh yes oh god yes" and in a couple of minutes more she did something that I had never seen before - she had an orgasm from being fucked anally. A minute later I came and we both laid down next to each other on the mattress.

She stared up at the roof of the cab for a bit and then she looked at me, "How long before you have to pull out?"

I thought about it and then told her that I really didn't have to be on the road till the morning. Then she said, "How would you like to get all of your money back and maybe make a little extra?"

I didn't know what to say to that so I just looked at her and she said, "I'm not kidding."

She had a determined look on her face so I asked, "What's this all about?"

She was quiet and stared at the roof for several seconds and then, "I'm not a prostitute. Oh, I know that by taking your money tonight and letting you do what you did I made myself one, but I have never done it before. What happened is that for the last five years now my husband has been begging me, actually begging me to have sex with another man. I would never do it because even though he swore up and down it was what he wanted most I didn't think he would be able to handle it if I did.

"Tonight we were at a party and half a dozen times he pointed at a guy and said "how about him? Why don't you take him out to the car and give him a little?' We stopped here on the way home for a bite to eat and I was using the phone to call the babysitter and tell her we were going to be a little later than we had planned. I had just enough to drink tonight to loosen me up and when you came up and hit on me I thought, why not? I'd never seen you before and I would never see you again so lets give hubby what he wants.

"That was him on the phone and I was right all along - he couldn't handle it. He called me a cheating bitch and a fucking whore and, well, you heard my side of it. The long and short of it is that he took off and left me here. I'm going to have to ask you to give me a ride home, but before I go there is something that I want to do."

I looked at her expectantly and she said, "He called me a fucking whore and I'm going to rub his nose in it. It might, no - it probably will - cost me my marriage, but right now I don't care. If I can use your sleeper for the rest of the night and if you will go out and find guys willing to fuck me for fifty bucks I'll give you all your money back and a third of whatever I make. Plus - you can fuck me as much as you want for free."

Elise had a busy night. She fucked thirty-one guys before the sun started peeking up over the horizon and I managed to do her three more times before she called it quits.

"I don't want to go into the truck stop and clean up; I want the bastard to see me just like this."

She gave me directions and as I pulled up in front of the house she asked me if I would mind waiting for a few minutes, "I might need to go to a motel or something."

Five minutes later she came out with a small suitcase and climbed up into the cab.

"Where to" I asked.

She shrugged and said, "I don't know. Where are you going?"

"Home to Denver."

"Want company?"

"What about your kids?"

"They are his from a previous marriage. He made it pretty plain that he doesn't want me around so it's hit the road for me."

"What will you do when we get to Denver?"

She looked at me, "Hopefully you liked what you got last night enough to let me stay with you for a couple of days while I try to figure it out."

"But I'm only home for five days and then I go on my next run."

"So I'll go with you."

"Not a good idea. You run into a lot of the same people at truck stops. We will always be running into those guys you did last night and to them you are a fifty dollar whore."

She stared out the window at the passing scenery and without looking at me said, "It will keep us in food and fuel money."

That was a year ago and Elise is still with me. Sometimes she rides with me and sometimes she stays home. When she rides with me it is a rare visit to a truck stop when Elise doesn't make five hundred bucks (she did raise her price to a hundred). I keep telling her that she doesn't have to do it, that I'm perfectly capable of taking care of her. She just smiles and says she has to do it to keep in touch with her roots. I keep after her to divorce her husband and marry me, but she won't do it. She called him and told him where to send the stuff she left behind and he begged her to forgive him and come home, but she said no. In an interesting twist he came to visit her while I was on a six day run and spent four days with her. Imagine that! Cheating on me with her own husband!

~~The End~~

WANT FREE COPIES OF MY BOOKS?

Just visit my blog and download free copies of my books:

awesomeauthors.org/justplainbob

My Publisher's Other BEST SELLING books on Amazon!!

Be My One and Only: Gay Romance

By: Erick Heslove

Michael had his entire life planned out – a great job, a wife, kids… and a lover to fulfill his homosexual needs.

The set-up seems perfect: Michael has his 'considerate' wife Macey and his devoted lover James. But Michael wants the same thing for his lover, and one fateful day, he urges James to look for a wife of his own.

By Michael's reckoning, James is not a hundred percent gay and having a wife and a child can give him the kind of happiness Michael feels with his family.

But James knows Michael is the only one for him and, constantly pressured by Mike to date women, the lovers are always at odds. Things only get worse when Michael's frustration at James begins to make their fights more hurtful and physical.

What will happen to their 'forever and beyond'?

I Never Kissed a Girl Before: Lesbian BDSM Erotica

By: Miranda Mars

When Laura meets tall, beautiful and gorgeous, but difficult Shontay, a fellow worker who just happens to be the daughter of the couple who live in the apartment above her own, she wanted her bad

Laura obsessed and she wants to and will take Shontay to bed, if only Shontay the ice queen would even look her way.

Shontay keeps putting Laura in her place, one that doesn't go anywhere near a bed. Determined to go where no girl has ever gone before with Shontay, can Laura finally come up with erotic schemes to get Shontay's affections?

A Girl Called Len: Falling in Love with a Stripper

By: <u>Kerry James</u>

Danny and Len grew up together; they played and went to the same school together... until the day when Danny's family was moving away to Exeter. Knowing they would never see each other again, Danny kissed Len. And that was goodbye. Or so they thought...

Ten years after the day that broke them apart, fate decides to intervene. Danny is now a computer programmer in post-war England with a precarious marriage. While on a course in London, he decides to go to a strip club only to get slapped by a shocking revelation. For right before his eyes, gyrating on stage among the strippers is Len!

All Night Arcade: Taboo Exhibitionist

By: <u>Jack Ryder</u>

Working the night shift at the all-night arcade brings Jake more "action" than he can handle. But does he like it? You bet he does!

Though married, Jake does not turn away Dixie and Fiona. Why should he when his own wife Dana also sleeps with men when he's at work? The video feed he watches from the secret cameras at home is proof of that.

But Dana has made a big mistake and asks him to punish her. Jake is planning on doing so, with Fiona. Can it salvage his marriage to Dana?

*For mature audiences ONLY.

Check out the list of all my books!

<u>The Prodigal Family: The Abbotts</u>

<u>Watching My Shared Wife</u>

<u>The Waitress and the Runaway Husband</u>

<u>Baiting Mr. Little</u>

<u>Too Hot for Henry</u>

<u>Chuck's Fantasy</u>

<u>The Redhead's Desires</u>

<u>Rescued at Riley's</u>

<u>His Every Fantasy</u>

<u>Open Mike Night</u>

<u>Pursuit for Revenge</u>

<u>Why Does He Do That?</u>

<u>Halloween & Drugs</u>

<u>Tracey</u>

<u>When Rob Met Kari</u>

<u>Becoming a Shared Wife, Vol. 1 –</u>
(Wife Sharing and Other Adventures)

<u>Becoming a Shared Wife, Vol. 2 –</u>
(Hazardous Wives)

<u>Becoming a Shared Wife, Vol. 3 –</u>
(Wives Who Stray)

Becoming a Shared Husband, Vol. 1 –

(Suck Me)

Becoming a Shared Husband, Vol. 2 –

(Husbands Who Stray)

Becoming a Shared Husband, Vol. 3 –

(Get even!)

Becoming a Shared Couple, Vol. 1 –

(Steamy Swingers)

Becoming a Shared Couple, Vol. 2 –

(The Share Thing)

Becoming a Shared Couple, Vol. 3 –

(Kathy is Wild)

Erotica Short Stories, Vol. 1 –

(Taboo Desires)

Erotica Short Stories, Vol. 2 –

(Nasty Steps)

Erotica Short Stories, Vol. 3 –

(Married But...)

Erotica Short Stories, Vol. 4 –

(Sizzling 10)

Erotica Short Stories, Vol. 5 –

(In My Wife's Panties)

Erotica Short Stories, Vol. 6 –

(Taboo Unlimited Desires)

Erotica Short Stories, Vol. 7 –

(XXX Stories)

Her Illicit Adventures

What I Want To Do To Her

Too Fun To Give Up

Creamed

Stepping Out

Hottest Wife

Naughty Wives

Deepest and Darkest

More Than She Can Take

Jennifer's Toes

The More The Sexier

Spice Up

Cyndi

Naughty And Nice

House Of Lovers

Hungry For More

Sweet Revenge

Turning Mommies Wild: The Carriage Tales

Bought And Used

Get Me Off

The Gambler

Gail's Price